(re)cycler

ALSO BY LAUREN MCLAUGHLIN
Cycler

(re)cycler

Lauren McLaughlin

Random House 🏠 New York

Library of Congress Cataloging-in-Publication Data
McLaughlin, Lauren.
(Re)cycler / Lauren McLaughlin. — 1st ed.
p. cm.
Summary: When eighteen-year-old Jill opts to move to New York with Ramie
rather than take a road trip with her boyfriend Tommy, all of their relationships
are shaken up as Jack, the boy she turns into for four days each month, finally
has the chance to get to know himself.
ISBN 978-0-375-85195-7 (trade pbk.) — ISBN 978-0-375-89292-9 (e-book)
[1. Interpersonal relations—Fiction. 2. Identity—Fiction. 3. Sex—Fiction.
4. Brooklyn (New York, N.Y.)—Fiction.] I. Title.
PZ7.M2238Rec 2009
[Fic]—dc22
2008043456

Printed in the United States of America
10 9 8 7 6 5 4 3 2 1
First Edition

for Andrew

(re)cycler

It was a night to remember for a handful of Winterhead
High seniors attending the annual prom at Karn Beach
Yacht Club last Saturday. According to witnesses, one
of the students arrived at the prom as an eighteen-
year-old boy and left as a girl.

"I swear to God," said senior Shelly Loman, "he was
like slow dancing with Ramie Boulieaux, and then he
collapsed on the floor."

Fellow senior Nicholas Tarzak claimed, "This dude
was all panting and shaking and stuff, and then he was—
oh, man, it was so weird."

Apparently the young man experienced an unspecified
medical problem, then transformed into local eighteen-
year-old Jill McTeague.

Ms. McTeague declined to comment on the alleged
incident, as did her parents, Helen and Richard McTeague.
Also declining to comment were Ramie Boulieaux and
newcomer Thomas Knutberg, who were seen escorting Ms.
McTeague from the yacht club.

"I know she wears a wig," said senior Jason Grimby.
"What's that about, right? I mean is she like a transvestite or something?"

Ms. McTeague had apparently experienced some teasing
in school a few weeks earlier about wearing a wig. She
is not known to have been a cross-dresser.

AUGUST 19

●

Jill

"I hope you know what you're doing, sweetie."

"Don't worry, Mom," I say. "I know exactly what I'm doing."

Mom doesn't believe me. And the fact that I can't stop nervously tugging on the ends of my wig doesn't help my case.

Mom and I are wandering through the luggage section at JCPenney because I have broken her best suitcase. Turns out you can't fit the entire contents of a bedroom into it. Live and learn, right?

"And when do you plan on telling us where you're going?" she asks. "Or are you going to leave us in the dark for good?"

"I'll tell you, Mom, just as soon as I figure it out." At the end of the aisle is a huge red Samsonite. I finger the lock on it. "I have two good options."

Mom snorts. She hates both of my options and never tires of reminding me how "unworkable" they both are. She thinks I should stay in Winterhead forever.

Trust me when I tell you, that is not an option.

I point to an even bigger blue Samsonite. "How about this one?" I say. "I think you could fit a body in there."

Mom looks at the price tag, then keeps walking.

"Mom," I say. "Suitcase or no suitcase, I'm still leaving. You realize that, right?"

When Mom stops walking, I prepare for another lecture about how deeply unready I am to exist without her constant supervision. But instead, she waves over a salesperson.

"We'll take this one," she says. She gestures toward the blue suitcase.

Later, while we're dragging the suitcase through the parking lot, I notice a car driving behind us very slowly. Inside are two sophomore boys from Winterhead High. I think one of them worked at the school snack shop and used to blush when I'd buy granola bars. Now they're both staring at me. I'm not an upperclassman to them anymore. I'm the girl who had that weird thing at the prom. You know, that *thing*?

I always want to confront people who look at me like that. I want to ask how they'd feel if they were in my shoes. But I never do. Instead, I hide behind my mother.

When she notices the car, she stops and bends over to get a good look at the boys with what I imagine is a lethal glare. The car speeds away.

"So, Mom?" I say. "In case you were wondering, *that's* why I have to leave."

Mom watches the car turn the corner at the Jiffy Lube. Then she pulls me close and kisses me on the head. "You know that I would do anything to protect you," she says. "Anything at all."

Of course I know that. If there's one thing that can be said of my mother, it's that in her mind there is no law superseding a mother's right to protect her daughter. She will take you down if you try to hurt me. I've come to respect that about her. Unfortunately, she can't take down the whole town of Winterhead, Massachusetts.

Okay, so here are my two options for escape. While I'm trying to squeeze my "essential" belongings into this new suitcase, *you* try to figure out which one is best.

The Ramie Option is to go with my best friend to New York City, where she is about to begin classes at the Fashion Institute of Technology.

The Tommy Option is to drive across the country with my boyfriend for a journey of self-discovery and much-delayed virginity termination.

Now, before you rush in with your verdict, keep in mind the following complicating factors:

1) Approximately four days every month, I turn into a boy named Jack.

2) Jack is dating Ramie. And by dating, I mean screwing on a regular, even daily, basis.

3) Jack is terrified of my boyfriend, Tommy, who is bisexual.

Go ahead, take your time. Create a spreadsheet, make some charts if it helps.

Not so easy, is it? Basically, I have to decide which one of us gets a sex life. You have to admit, it's a bit more challenging than the decisions most eighteen-year-olds have to make. Most of the eighteen-year-olds I know are busy trying to decide which posters to put up in their dorm rooms.

But I'm trying not to be a complainer. Complaining solves nothing. Plus it creates scowl lines between your eyebrows, which I am against.

It's D-day. Tommy will be here any minute. Mom's been pacing outside my door all morning. And I still haven't decided where or who I'm escaping *to*.

"Jill?" Mom says. She comes to my doorway with her hands on her hips. "You need to tell us. *Now*. Your father's going crazy."

"*Going?*" I say.

I hear a car horn outside. Rushing to the window, I spot Tommy's silver Prius pulling into the driveway.

Mom dries the corners of her eyes with a tissue. "I don't know if you're doing this for dramatic effect, Jill, but—"

"Mom, please."

I want to tell her that everything will be okay, but the truth is, I am as lost in this sea of fear and doubt as she is. The only thing I know for sure is that I have to leave. When I open my mouth to say something reassuring, though, the only thing that comes out is a big sob.

"Come here," Mom says, her voice ragged with pain.

I rush into her arms and let her hug me in a way she hasn't since I was a little girl.

"I hate this," she says.

"Me too."

I can hear Dad downstairs, asking Tommy to wait in the living room; then his footsteps rise up the stairs. Mom clings to me for as long as she can, then lets Dad have one final hug. Dad's as nutty-looking as ever, with his long hair and guru beard. But I think he must have showered for the occasion, because he doesn't smell nearly as bad as he usually does.

"Bye, Dad," I say.

"No, sweetheart." He kisses the top of my head. "It's not goodbye, it's see you later."

Tommy's silver Prius is spotless and freshly carvac'ed. Plus it smells like a new car because of the new-car air freshener hanging from the rearview mirror.

I point to it. "That's symbolic."

"Mmmm-hmmm," he says.

"You know, like new beginnings?" I say.

He nods as he drives us to the end of Trask Road.

Tommy is his same beautiful self, his longish brown hair just skirting his broad, bony shoulders. How I love those shoulders. How I'll *miss* those shoulders if I don't take the Tommy Option.

I haven't decided yet.

As we leave Trask Road and my old life behind, Tommy taps the steering wheel nervously. I know what he's thinking. He's thinking, Enough is enough, Jill. Am I dropping you off in New York or taking you west with me? Make up your mind, for crying out loud.

But he's too decent to push. He knows how hard this is for me.

We drive in silence for a while, Main Street already showing the early signs of autumn in the colorful decay of leaves. I crack the window and let the crisp air slice into the car.

"How'd *your* mom take it?" I ask.

"All right," he says. "She was an army brat, remember? She's never lived in the same place for more than a few years. She thinks wanderlust runs in the family."

"Right," I say. "Hey, Tommy?"

"Yeah?"

"Thanks," I say.

"For what?" he says. "My car is your car."

"Not for that," I say.

As we near Cherry Street, he slows down, then stops to wait for the oncoming traffic to clear. "For what?"

"For being, you know, so cool about everything. After the prom."

"The prom," he says. "Did something happen at the prom?"

I laugh, and he takes my hand.

"You're taking the Ramie Option," he says. "Aren't you?"

It's only when he says it that I realize I've made up my mind.

"I think I have to," I say. "It's just . . ."

"It's Jack," he says. "Right?"

I nod. "Tommy, if Jack ever woke up in a Motel 6 next to you, I don't know what he'd do."

Tommy laughs darkly. "I can guess."

"I'm really sorry," I say.

"It's okay," Tommy says. "I had a feeling that's what you'd decide."

When the traffic clears, he turns left down Cherry Street.

"Thanks for driving us," I say.

"New York's on the way," he says. "Besides, I want to get as much of you as I can."

When he steals a look at me with those penetrating brown eyes, it feels like the first time I saw him in calculus class, and all I want to do is stay in that car with him forever.

When we pull into Ramie's driveway, she's sitting on the front porch twisting her wild black bramble hair into a knot. She's wearing overalls and a big white ruffled shirt, neither of which can mask her absurdly bombshell-ish bod. As soon as she spots us, she jumps up, squeals in delight, then runs inside to get her stuff.

I turn to Tommy. "You know, you could always stay with us in Brooklyn if you want. I'm sure Ramie won't mind."

Tommy shuts off the car. "Jill," he says. "I've been saving up for this road trip since middle school."

"I know," I say.

He interlaces his fingers with mine. "It's only one year."

Only?

"You're sure you don't want to come?" he says. "Are you positively and *deeply* sure?"

No! I want to scream. The only thing I *am* sure of is that I want to drive westward with Tommy Knutson forever. I want to tell him I love him, then lose my virginity in the Arizona desert. On an Aztec blanket at sunset, with a coyote howling in the distance. All summer long I've been fantasizing that scene. That *exact* scene.

But then Jack went and wrote me that letter.

"It's not too late to change your mind," Tommy says. "You haven't told Ramie yet, have you?"

"No," I say. "But listen to this." I dig Jack's letter out of my backpack. The handwriting is neater than usual. Plus I found six different drafts of it in the wastebasket when I woke up. He put a lot of thought into it.

"Are you ready?" I ask.

He nods.

" 'Dear Jill,' " I read. " 'I know you have a hard decision to make and I really appreciate how seriously you're considering my interests. We've had our differences in the past, and I'm sorry for the pain I've caused you. Despite everything that's happened, I have faith in your inherent decency. That's why I know you'll do the right thing. Love, Jack.' "

I fold the letter neatly and return it to my backpack.

"Wow," Tommy says. "That's either incredibly beautiful or really manipulative."

"I know," I say.

I don't tell Tommy about the earlier drafts of this letter, which articulated in not-so-beautiful language just how much Jack despises Tommy (variously referred to as Knutcase, Knutjob, and Knutsack). Jack has near-perfect recall of my life, including my everything-but-actual-sex life with Tommy, to which he objects vehemently. In contrast, my memory of Jack's life is spotty at best. Ramie fills me in, though, and one thing is crystal clear: Jack and Tommy will never be friends.

"What could I do?" I tell Tommy. "Jack has lived his whole life trapped in a bedroom."

"True."

"He kind of deserves a break, don't you think?"

"I guess," he says. Then he lays those penetrating eyes on me. "So, what about us?"

Us.

Us is a subject we've both been avoiding, though it's hung like a cloud over us all summer long.

"Do you want to . . . ," he says. "I mean, should we . . ."

"We can still talk," I say. "It's not like you're driving to the moon."

"Yeah," he says. "But should we, like, you know . . ."

"Break up?" I say.

"Do you want to?"

"No!" I say. "I mean, do you?"

He shrugs. "Not really," he says. "But what should we . . ."

"Um," I say. "I don't know. Do you want to maybe . . ."

"Should we just play it by ear?" he says.

Play it by ear?

"What do you think?" he says.

What I think is, *What the hell does play it by ear mean?*

He squeezes my hand.

"Yes," I hear myself say. "Play it by ear. Sure. Yeah. That sounds good, I guess."

He looks down. "Okay."

Just then Ramie crashes through her screen door with a giant suitcase on wheels.

Tommy leans over and kisses me on the forehead. "We'll play it by ear, then." He presses his lips together in a business-like smile.

"Sure," I say.

He pops the trunk, then gets out of the car to help Ramie.

I get out too and call my mom to tell her I've chosen the Ramie Option. She's not happy about it. She and Ramie have, at best, a nonaggression pact. But she does admit that it's the "lesser evil," since, at the very least, it means I'll be sleeping in an apartment and not with a bisexual boy.

For a second I'm tempted to ask her if she knows what Play It by Ear means, but I doubt they had Play It by Ear in the Dark Ages when she was dating, and anyway, I am not in the habit of asking my mother for relationship advice. For one thing, she and my dad don't even sleep on the same story in my house. For another, the last time I took Mom's advice, I wound up dangling by a pair of skis from a sadistic J-bar. Don't ask. It was ugly.

When I close my cell phone, I look at Ramie and Tommy struggling to make everything fit into the trunk. Then I look over both of their heads at the giant maple tree in Ramie's front yard. That tree has played a surprisingly large role in my life.

Two and a half hours later, midway to New York City, Ramie makes us pull over at a rest stop so she can pee out the half gallon of iced green tea she's drunk. It must be the excitement of becoming "the next Alexander McQueen" that's made her so thirsty.

While Tommy and Ramie use the facilities, I get out to stretch my legs and collect my thoughts. Now that I've made up my mind about where I'm going, everything's moving so fast. I've gained a New York address and, depending on the precise definition of Play It by Ear, possibly lost a boyfriend.

In the grass strip between two rows of parked cars, three little kids are play fighting with plastic light sabers while their parents rearrange their bags in the trunk. Those kids don't know how lucky they are. All they have to do is whack each other with plastic until Mom and Dad put them back in the car. Mom and Dad will decide where they're going and how to get there. Mom and Dad will replace the batteries as needed, tuck them in at night, and make all their Big Scary Decisions for them. I bet they've never even heard the words "play it by ear."

After a few minutes Ramie runs out of the food court and plants herself next to me with a bag of French fries.

"Okay," she says. "Before he gets back, tell me everything."

"There's nothing to tell," I say. "We're playing it by ear."

"What does that mean?"

"I was hoping you'd know."

"How would I know?" she says. "Are you breaking up?"

"I don't know."

"How can you not know? Are you going to have sex with him tonight?"

I shrug.

"Jill," she says. "What are you waiting for? A sign from the heavens? Oh, that reminds me. Are your cycles still going wonky?"

"They're just a little bit irregular," I say. "That's all."

"Damn," she says. "I was hoping we could keep a calendar so I'd know *exactly* how long I have to wait between conjugal visits."

I grab two of her French fries and shove them into my

mouth. I'm working on feigning nonchalance over the fact that my body spends four days every month screwing Ramie's brains out.

"You know," she says, inching close to me. "Tonight's the perfect night. It'll be all tragic and beautiful. I'll wear earplugs, I swear. I won't listen."

"Liar."

"Ooh." She whacks me on the shoulder. "So you *are* doing it tonight!" She takes out her cell phone.

"What are you doing?" I ask.

"Texting Daria," she says.

I grab her phone. "What is *wrong* with you!"

"Jill," she says. "Don't be a tease. Are you or aren't you? Daria's concerned."

"*Daria's* concerned?"

"She thinks you're building it up too much, like the Tower of Babylon."

"I'm not building it up. And isn't it the Tower of Babel?"

"I don't know." Ramie swipes her cell phone back.

"And what does the Tower of Babel have to do with anything?" I say. "That's completely the wrong metaphor. I mean, if anything, Sodom and Gomorrah."

"What is this, Bible study all of a sudden?" Ramie says. "We're talking about your sex life. Oh, I'm sorry. I meant your complete absence of a sex life."

"Don't start."

"Jill," she says. "All I'm saying is that maybe you should try—just as an experiment, you don't have to commit to it forever—but maybe you could try being a little bit less of a prude for one night. Would it kill you?"

"I'm not a prude," I say.

"Define prude."

"Define slut," I say.

"That's exactly what a prude would say."

"Tommy and I have done stuff," I say. "Lots of stuff."

Ramie snorts dismissively.

"We have," I say. "But come on, Rames, be honest. If you were me, knowing how I feel about him, would you have sex with him tonight?"

Ramie nods aggressively.

"But he's leaving tomorrow," I say. "Wouldn't that technically make me a one-night stand?"

"Mal," she says. "You're so regressive. And anyway, when you've been doing foreplay all summer long, I don't think it qualifies as a one-night stand. Come on, Jill, he's your dream guy. How much more perfect could it be?"

"It would be a little more perfect if he weren't leaving tomorrow. Ramie, I don't even know if he loves me."

"Have you told him you love him?" she says.

I shake my head.

"Of course," she says. "He has to say it first, right?"

"I just don't want to feel like a fool," I say.

"There's a fine line between fool and virgin," she says around a mouthful of French fries. "And anyway, where is it written that love has to come before sex? I didn't love Jack before I had sex with him. We had tons of sex before—"

"Ramie." I put my hand over her mouth. "Not now."

Ramie and Jack's sex life is not my favorite subject. I accept it. But I do not need all the slurpy details.

Ramie's eyes flick to the left.

I remove my hand from her mouth and see Tommy walking straight for us with a water bottle.

"Hey," he says. He hands me the bottle. "Are you guys talking about me again?"

"Hmm." I inspect the bottle. "Do they add vanity to this stuff now?"

Tommy takes the bottle back. "Right. Like you guys don't talk about me all the time." He takes a sip. "Come on. Let's make up some time."

There is one thing you should probably know about New York City, in case you ever decide to move here. Actually, there are plenty of things you should know, but the first thing that will make itself deeply, one could say painfully, clear to you is this:

It's not like *Sex and the City* or even *Gossip Girl*.

Picture the ugliest clapboard three-story house sheathed in pale blue vinyl siding with fake marble steps and two plastic columns at the entrance.

Can you see it?

That's our apartment building.

Emerging from the broken screen door is a fat man with a comb-over, wearing a pit-stained T-shirt and blue chinos, which do not quite meet over his domelike belly. He looks like an extra from a Mafia movie.

"I thought you said there was only two a youse," he says.

His name, to my great surprise, is not Vito Marinara or Tony Fettucini, but rather Paul Harkin. He's our landlord, and he lives on the bottom floor.

Ramie steps right up to him and shakes his hand. "Hi. I'm Ramie Boulieaux. This is Jill McTeague."

He shakes my hand dismissively, then looks at Tommy as if he were an uninvited guest at a wedding.

"I'm not moving in," Tommy says. "I'm just passing through."

Mr. Harkin looks him up and down suspiciously, then motions with his head for us to follow him inside.

"Is the car safe here?" Tommy asks.

Mr. Harkin shrugs, then takes us up to the third floor.

As he shows us around the furnished two-bedroom apartment, he lets us know that the house has been in his family for three generations and that they do not allow long-term guests or pets of any kind. Also, no parties, no drugs, and "no hammering nails in the wall to hang art or nothin.' "

Above the mantel, there is, for our convenience and enjoyment, an oil painting of a dog and a cat facing each other in what might be an epic battle or the beginning of an interspecies romance. There is no fireplace, only a slight protrusion in the plaster where it was sloppily bricked over.

The place is dark and smells faintly of paint. The furniture looks like the kind of stuff a church group would donate after a hurricane: mismatched cushions on the sofa, a coffee table with a taped-on leg.

"It's beautiful," Ramie says.

"You're paying cash, right?" Mr. Harkin mumbles.

Ramie removes an envelope from her purse and hands it to him. "First and last."

By six-thirty, we've gotten everything unloaded from the car and unpacked in our teeny tiny bedrooms. Tommy and I are exhausted, but Ramie drags us out to "scope the hood."

Our street, Edgar Avenue, features an endless row of tacky three-story homes, with cars crammed so tightly at curbside I'm not sure how anyone gets in or out without an airlift.

"It's not what I expected," Tommy says in a bout of extreme generosity.

"I thought you lived in New York once," Ramie says.

"Long Island," he says. "Not Brooklyn."

"Did you know," Ramie says, "that Greenpoint is a Polish neighborhood?"

"I thought this was Williamsburg," I say.

"Technically, no," she says. "We couldn't afford Williamsburg. Ooh!" She points to a green canvas awning that reads Wlskazhsky or Wslzielkkasxy or something.

"A Polish deli!" she says. "Let's get some kielbasa, then go sit up on the roof."

Tommy and I look at each other doubtfully, but Ramie grabs us both by the hand and drags us inside.

Ten minutes later, kielbasa in hand, we're standing on our rooftop gazing at a handful of brightly colored lawn chairs, plus a broken exercise bike and a deeply frightening giant stuffed panda covered in soot.

"Wow!" Ramie says. "You've got to see this." She motions for us to join her on the other side of the central water tower, which juts out of the roof.

And there before us, laid out like a glittering strand of jewels against the dusky sky, is Manhattan. The Empire State Building, the Chrysler Building, and thousands of others shine back at us as if to say "Hello there! Welcome to New York!"

The three of us rest our elbows on the four-foot wall and stare in awe.

"Wow is right," I say. I look at Tommy. How could he want to leave such an amazing place? What could he possibly find on the road to San Francisco that competes with this?

"Can't you smell the energy?" Ramie says.

I breathe in deeply. "Yeah," I say.

"Actually . . ." Tommy points to a pair of silver domelike structures in the distance. "I think that's a sewage treatment plant."

"Oh." Ramie peels herself away to look over the edge on the other side of the roof. "Hey," she says. "There's a homeless guy picking through our trash cans." She looks over at us, all excited.

I flash her the thumbs-up. Then I return to that glittering necklace. "Tommy," I say. "I don't think I've ever seen anything so beautiful."

"Hmm," he says. "I have."

He looks at me and fiddles with the ends of my wig.

"Yeah," I say, looking back at him. "Me too."

●

By ten o'clock we've figured out exactly where we are on Ramie's map of Brooklyn, and yes, those two silver domes *are* a sewage treatment plant. Ramie heads out to explore Bedford Avenue, which is "the capital of do-it-yourself street fashion," according to some magazine she keeps quoting. This leaves Tommy and me alone in the apartment.

Despite its being our last night together, I still have not decided whether or not to have sex with him. Why do all of my Big Scary Decisions have to come within a few hours of each other? Why can't everything slow down?

After showers (separate showers, FYI), Tommy and I sit together on the sofa with its mismatched cushions. Even with the very down-market nature of its furnishings, the apartment does have a kind of charm. A small, dark, cramped charm.

"I think I'm going to like it here," I say.

"Good," he says. "Promise you won't get a cat, though."

"Why?"

He lies down on the couch and puts his damp head in my lap. "I don't know," he says. "There's something not right about single girls with cats."

The way he refers to me as a single girl makes my stomach turn over.

"Well, Ramie's not exactly single," I say.

Tommy looks up at me. I don't count the Mississippis anymore when he does this.

"Ramie's a lucky girl," he says.

"Yeah, I know. Jack's amazing and wonderful and an incredible lover. I've heard. Believe me, I've heard."

"So have I," he says. "When she's finished telling you, she tells me."

"Is that weird for you?" I say. "You know, because we're, like . . . you know . . ."

He shakes his head in the negative. "Yes."

"Really?" I say.

He nods while saying "No."

"Tommy!"

"Maybe?"

His hand creeps under my T-shirt.

I grab it and hold it steady. "Subject changer."

He yanks his hand free and slides it up the back of my shirt. "I don't know if it's weird or not," he says. "And I don't really care. All I know is this summer has been amazing, and I wish you were coming with me." His hand drifts back to my stomach and begins to wander upward. "But I guess this is it."

"It?" I say.

He nods. "It." He lifts his head from my lap and kisses me.

I kiss him back, and within seconds we're on my bed in a flurry of flying clothes. This is how it always goes with us. We'll be walking through the dunes having an innocent conversation, or sitting on a blanket reading books to each other, when all of a sudden we're down to our underwear. It's not that we don't do foreplay. Technically, foreplay is *all* we do. It's just that we do it very fast. It's like a sudden hunger overtakes us and all we can do is obey its demands. Tommy never pressures me to go all the way, but he's made it abundantly clear that he's up for it. In fact, he's been up for it ever since that first day in calculus when he laid those gorgeous brown eyes on me and we began a long, smoldering campaign of sticky eyes. I have to admire the ease of his lustfulness as well as his patience.

Now, though, in the dingy light from the ceramic poodle lamp in my bedroom (yes, I said ceramic poodle lamp), things have a heightened now-or-neverness to them. By the time Tommy and I have flung away all fabric barriers between us, I'm frozen. And my wig's come slightly loose.

When I readjust it, he grabs my hand gently. "You can take it off," he says. "I don't mind."

It's sweet, but I'm not ready to feel sexy beneath the boyish fringe of my overgrown crew cut. I'm ready for very few of the things life is throwing at me these days. I secure an errant hairpin and keep the wig in place. Part of me wants to forget the Big Scariness of this Decision and let my body have its way. My body doesn't worry about complicated, abstract stuff. It's a simple animal. But the other part of me, you know, the head part? That part wants everything to . . .

Slow.

The heck.

Down.

"It's okay," he says. "Whatever you want." He kisses me softly. "What *do* you want?"

"I want . . ."

He kisses me again.

I want to know that he loves me.

His lips caress my cheek.

I *don't* want to Play It by Ear.

His lips wander down my neck.

I'd much prefer to Stay Faithful to Each Other.

"Stop," I tell him.

He looks up at me expectantly.

The words "I love you" are somewhere on their journey from the pit of my soul to the tip of my tongue.

"Yes?" he says.

But they never make it out.

"I'm sorry," I say.

"It's okay." He kisses my forehead. "I don't want to rush you."

But everything is rushed now. Time is ticking by, and I feel like I'm running in quicksand.

Tommy slides off of me and settles his head on his hand. "You don't want to?"

I do. I just can't bring myself to say it.

"Don't worry," he says. "When you're ready, you'll know."

I hope he's right, because I don't feel like I know anything anymore.

"Hey, Jill," he says. "About tomorrow. When I go?"

My throat dries up.

He takes a deep, nervous breath. "I'm really afraid of falling apart, so I'm just going to get up early and sneak out, okay?"

"But . . . why?"

"I want this to be our last moment together. Right now. Like this." He puts his arms around me. "Not some horrible good-bye."

That's when it finally hits me. This is *not* see you later. This is goodbye.

"Sure," I say. "That's a good idea."

"Thank you." He inches down and nestles his face in my neck.

His long arms wrap around me and his long legs cross with mine. We hold each other silently in the poodle's dim light, Tommy's head growing heavy on my shoulder. We lie like that in silence for a while. I shiver, not from the cold, but from the fear that each decision I have made is the wrong one. And none of them can be reversed.

Eventually Ramie's keys jingle in the lock. Slowly and quietly, she tiptoes down the hall and stands outside my bedroom door.

"So cool," she whispers just outside the door. "You're going to love it here. Two-dollar pizza." She tiptoes to her own room across the creaky floor.

When I reach for the poodle's cord to kill the light, Tommy stirs, then settles.

"Tommy?" I whisper.

But he's asleep now.

"I love you," I whisper.

In the distance, a siren wails.

In the morning, when I open my eyes, the first thing I notice is the empty space on the other side of my bed. The second is a Post-it stuck to the nose of the ceramic poodle. Written across it in bold blue Sharpie are the words "I love you too."

●

"I don't understand," Ramie says.

"Neither do I."

Ramie and I are sitting in a red vinyl booth at a diner where no one speaks English and a lot of cabbage is boiled. I have Tommy's Post-it note gripped firmly in hand.

When the waitress comes over, Ramie orders scrambled eggs and bacon for both of us by pointing at the menu. "We should deeply learn Polish," she whispers. She cocks her head to the side. "Jill, are you okay?"

"I just don't understand, Ramie." I hold up Tommy's note. "What does this mean?"

She takes the note away from me and sticks it on the table. "It means he loves you."

"But . . ."

"But nothing, Jill. He loves you, and you should have had sex with him."

I stare at her dumbly.

"Oh." She reaches across the table and grabs my hand. "I'm sorry. It's deeply not the time for tough love, is it?"

I shake my head.

The waitress wordlessly deposits two mugs of coffee on the table.

I slump over my cup, pour some cream into it, then take a sip. "That's disgusting."

"I forgot to tell you," she says. "They put milk in their coffee here instead of cream."

"Why?"

Ramie shrugs. "To punish Red Sox fans?" She smiles hopefully.

But I'm in no mood to be cheered.

The waitress brings us a plate of white toast with some plastic packets of grape jelly.

"I blew it," I say. "Didn't I?"

Ramie sighs.

I slump back in the red vinyl seat and stare at the street scene beyond the diner's large window. There's a fruit-and-vegetable market and an offtrack betting establishment, plus some middle-aged women with wonderful cheekbones pushing shopping trolleys. It seems strange that this is my new home, my "hood." One day soon, this will all be familiar. I wonder what that will feel like.

I take a bite of toast. "Sorry to be such a drag."

"You can be a drag if you want," she says. "But only for today."

"All right," I say.

But I don't think one day will cover it. All summer long I was saving myself until I knew for sure that Tommy loved me. Now I think he always did but was waiting for me to say it first.

"Jill," Ramie says. "You're spiraling."

"Huh?"

"It's okay to obsess about Tommy," she says. "Just do it out loud. Don't sink into yourself."

"Okay," I say.

But when the eggs come, I poke at them in silence while sneaking glances at the upside-down writing on Tommy's note. I wonder where he is right now and if he has any regrets. Is he driving down the highway wondering if he got it all wrong too?

Probably not. Tommy's at the beginning of an amazing journey, a journey he's dreamed of since middle school.

So is Ramie, for that matter. They both have bright, shiny futures to look forward to. They can dream big and have exciting adventures.

Not me. Surviving high school with my secret intact was all I ever hoped for.

And I didn't even get that. Not that I'm complaining.

"One year," Ramie says.

"Huh?"

"He'll be back. You'll see."

I nod, but I'm not so sure.

"And you know," she says. "A lot can happen to a girl in one year. Especially in this city."

I cringe through another sip of bitter coffee. "What?" I say. "Like getting mugged?"

Ramie pushes the tin pitcher toward me. "Just add more milk," she says. "And by the way, New York is one of the safest cities in the world."

I fill my cup all the way to the lip, then lean over and have a tepid sip.

"See?" she says. "It's not so bad."

I shrug. I like my coffee from Dunkin' Donuts. With three sugars and a lot of cream.

"Who knows?" Ramie says. "When Tommy comes back—"

"*If* Tommy comes back."

Ramie nods. "If he comes back, he may not even recognize you."

I have to admit, there's something appealing about that scenario.

september 7

●

Jack

Good morning, ladies and gentlemen. Have you enjoyed the journey thus far? No? A little gloomy? A bit of a letdown with old Tommy Knutson? I hear you. But cut the girl some slack. She's been a prude for a long time. I'm doing my best to inspire her with my feats of sexual daring, but old habits die hard.

Anyway, on this end of the cycle it has been one heck of a ride since the day Jill found herself sprawled on the floor of the Karn Beach Yacht Club in a man's suit and no idea how she got there.

"Um, Ramie, um, is this, like, the prom?"

I won't lie. I had myself a guilty chuckle when I woke up and found that memory in the old thinkbox. Oh, come on, the girl had it coming. She "deeply" had it coming. But despite the poetical nature of that particular nugget of justice, I did not spend the summer wallowing in Jill's pain. I had my own stuff going on.

Lots and lots of it, in fact.

Now, contrary to Jill's complaints, I have not devoted my hard-won freedom *exclusively* to the sacred task of making sweet, sweet love to Ramie Boulieaux. All right, it's number one on my agenda, but there's been other stuff. Stuff like riding the roller coaster at Canobie Lake Park and swimming in the Atlantic Ocean. Have you ever swum in the Atlantic Ocean? With your own body and your own senses? Who knew it actually tasted like salt? I mean, sure I *knew*, but I didn't *know*. You know?

Novel Sensations. *That's* what I'm about these days.

Today's first Novel Sensation is the disorienting feeling of waking up in a strange bed with the sound of traffic through the window and a ceramic poodle smiling down at me. Novel Sensation number two is rushing to my girlfriend's bedroom for a surprise morning snuggle. And Novel Sensation number three is the sight of a one-armed mannequin standing guard over her otherwise empty bedroom.

A quick scan of Jilltime reveals that Ramie's in class today from ten to four, so I lie down in her bed for a few seconds to absorb her residual aroma. Then I mosey into the living room for an inspection of my new home. It's small. It's dark. The dominant design motif is duct tape. But you know what, it's mine. Well, *ours* anyway. There is a locked door that leads to the outside world, and I have the key.

Just to be sure, I turn all three metal locks and peer into the hallway. I could run up and down those stairs in my underwear if I wanted to. Who's going to stop me?

That's when I feel Novel Sensation number four: total

freedom. I take a big lung-expanding breath of it. Then I cough it back out because the apartment still smells of paint.

I head to the kitchen and make a quick peanut butter sandwich. Then I sit on Jill's bed to plan my day. Did I say *Jill's* bed? I meant *my* bed. I've got to stop thinking I'm an intruder in Jill's life. This is *my* life now. This is Jack's bed.

On the dresser is an envelope with my name on it, and inside are fifty bucks, a MetroCard, and a note printed on some insurance company's letterhead.

Jill's always leaving me little notes like this, even though she *knows* I remember everything. Like I said, old habits die hard.

"Hi, Jack," the note reads. "I've registered with a temp agency and worked out a budget for us. The $50 I've enclosed is *all you can spend.* Sorry it's not more, but things are really expensive here. We don't have our own Internet or cable, but you can jump on the 'NatBitch' airport most of the time. Welcome to New York. I hope you like it. Be careful. Love, Jill."

I throw on some jeans, then stuff the money in my back pocket.

Be careful? Is she kidding?

It's an overcast, sixty-degree September day. Forgive me, but I'm still wowed by the Novel Sensation of weather. When the sun bursts suddenly from behind a cloud, I have to stop at the corner to catch my breath. The feel of sudden heat on cool skin is bewildering and kind of sexual. I savor it for a few seconds, then follow the smell of cut grass. I am familiar with this smell, having experienced it on many occasions through my bedroom window in Winterhead. But it's different when you can follow it like a road map to secret treasure. The sweet, fertile aroma leads me to McCarren Park, a green oasis that divides Greenpoint (all kielbasa shops and cheap shoes) from Williamsburg (hipsters, expensive coffee). The park itself is bigger than anything in Winterhead, with a running track, a kids' playground, two dog runs, and three baseball diamonds. Right now it's mostly empty except for some people jogging around the track.

I head toward Williamsburg armed only with a vague plan to buy a coffee somewhere. Why?

Because I can.

I have an inkling that the world beyond Brooklyn is a great and terrible place, with even more wonders to behold than the squeak of playground swings or the mysterious flight pattern of pigeons. But the only way I can manage the brain-challenging bigness of it all is to take it one Novel Sensation at a time.

After a few blocks, in need of a break from the sensorial onslaught, I slip into a dingy little bar called Spitfire. For no other reason than the fact that I have never done so before, I order a Scotch. The bartender doesn't even card me. He just points to the door and tells me to come back in ten years.

And I thought underage drinking was the nation's number one scourge. That's what the guidance counselors were always telling Jill and her classmates.

At any rate, it would be foolish to spend my limited time allotment in a drunken haze. I need my senses working at full capacity if I'm going to cram a lifetime of stuff into four-twenty-eighths of a life.

Wow. Four-twenty-eighths of a life. I have to stop for a second because that is one dark little mind burp. I mean when you actually do the math, it doesn't add up to much, does it?

This wouldn't have bothered me so much when I was a prisoner in Jill's bedroom. Back then, time moved with agonizing slowness. Sometimes it moved so slowly, I'd stare out that window and pray for oblivion. Now there never seems to be *enough* time.

But you know what? I am not about spiraling into existential funks. Jill does enough of that for both of us. I shake myself out of it, then head toward Bedford Avenue, where, if Jilltime memory serves, the pretty, happy people are.

Eventually I wander into this little joint called Dexter's. I remember from Jilltime that Dexter's is usually crowded at night with cool kids nursing cans of Pabst Blue Ribbon (ironically, of course), but during the day it's only modestly populated by coffee drinkers. Plus you don't have to be twenty-one just to enter the stinkin' place.

I order a coffee from the bartender, whose name is Joel and who is an aspiring screenwriter. He told this to Jill while serving her a ginger ale one night, and they bonded over the fact that they both have jobs they hate. Jill, the nitwit, didn't even pick up on the fact that Joel was flirting with her. She's still saving herself for Knutsack, the Arizona desert, and that howling coyote.

Whatev.

I take my coffee and find a seat alone at a small table covered with someone's abandoned newspaper. As I glance around the place, with its clusters of twos and threes of people, I feel suddenly self-conscious about being alone. Then it occurs to me that the only people I even know, other than Ramie, are Daria (nice, but kind of a dingbat and nowhere near Brooklyn), my parents (total psychos who locked me in a room), and Tommy Knutson (need I elaborate?).

I take a sip of coffee and come to the conclusion that I'd better get myself some friends. You know, people who can keep me entertained while Ramie's in class. It's possible, however, that my "upbringing," if you can call it that, has deprived me of the necessary people skills required to make friends. But, I figure, nothing ventured, nothing gained, right?

I scan the joint in search of possible targets. There are a couple of guys deep in confab over in the corner, a long-haired dude—who reminds me of Dad—slumped over a bottle of beer at the bar, and a smattering of girls. Then my eye lands on this guy right behind me, sitting alone at a big table by the window and scribbling in a notebook. He's tall and scrawny, with messy hair, but he doesn't *look* like a psycho. Plus he's drinking a tall glass of orange juice, which speaks well of his attitude toward nutrition. I must be staring, because he looks up from his notebook and squints at me.

"Hey," I say.

"Hey," he says back.

And we're off.

"What's your name?" I say.

"Larson," he says. "Why?"

"I'm Jack," I say. "Jack McTeague."

He looks around and nods evasively. Then he returns to his notebook.

"What are you drinking?" I say.

"Um, dude, like, I'm not gay or anything."

"Me neither," I say. "What are you writing? Is that homework?"

"Kind of," he says.

I keep staring at him.

He sighs. "It's for a comp class."

"What's that?"

"Composition?" he says. "Like writing?"

"I've heard of it."

"I'm supposed to keep a journal."

"About what?"

He looks around nervously. "Like, life?"

"Your own?"

He nods.

"Sounds fun," I say. "Can you lie?"

"Um," he says. "That's kind of defeating the purpose. I'm supposed to write for half an hour a day without taking my pen off the page."

"Oh," I say. "Did I just mess that up for you?"

"Kind of."

"Sorry."

Larson sighs, then closes his notebook. "It's all right," he says. "It's a gut class. All I need is a C. Are you a student?"

I shake my head. He keeps looking at me, presumably in anticipation of a more data-rich answer. I'm tempted to improvise a story about being an entrepreneur or an import-export guy, but I'm a bad liar, and anyway I don't know what either of those things are.

"I'm kind of . . . between jobs?" I say. "I just moved here."

"Where from? Wait, don't tell me. Midwest?"

"Massachusetts."

"Damn," he says. "I'm usually good at accents. I'm majoring in linguistics."

Wow, I think, *that sounds unbelievably boring.* "Mind if I join you?" I say.

He shrugs. "I'm meeting some guys in a few minutes, but sure."

I take my coffee over and sit across the table from him. "So," I say, "what guys are you meeting?"

He laughs.

"What?" I say. "Am I being too nosy?"

He keeps laughing. "No. It's . . . um . . ."

"What?"

"You're kind of strange," he says.

"You don't know the half of it, pal."

"Really?"

I nod, but I don't elaborate, because mystery is cool. "So what do you do for fun around here?"

"Fun?" he says. "Um, I don't know. Meet girls. Get drunk."

"Really?"

"Yeah," he says. "What do *you* do for fun?"

I take a sip of my coffee. "To be honest, Larson, I've spent the last two months mostly screwing my girlfriend."

"Really?"

I nod. "I'm getting really good at it too. She can't keep her hands off of me. I'm kind of a love god."

All of a sudden, a shadow is cast by this little blond string bean who stands at the edge of our table. "Who's the love god?" he asks.

Larson looks up. "Yo, Perm. What's up?" They do a funky jive handshake.

I extend my hand to him. "Jack," I say.

He doesn't shake my hand. He just stares at me with squinty eyes. The bits of yellow hair poking from beneath his little hat are bone straight and obviously bleached.

A few seconds later a tall black dude wearing an old Journey concert T-shirt slides into the chair next to me. "Hey," he says. "I'm Alvarez." He shakes my hand, then clings to a large cup of coffee.

Perm remains standing at the edge of the table, looking down on me as if I were a turd dropped from the heavens. "Larson," he says, while looking at me. It's a neat trick. Very menacing. "You've got the chart?"

Larson looks at me sheepishly. "Anyway," he says, "these are the guys I was talking about. It was nice to meet you."

I nod for a few seconds before I realize he's asking me to leave. So much for making friends, I guess. I grab my coffee and head back to my solitary table.

Is it my baggy jeans? I wonder. *My non-ironic T-shirt?*

When I sneak a glance at their table, Larson is shrugging and rolling his eyes as Perm gesture-queries him as to the meaning of my apparently unacceptable intrusion into their important meeting.

Fine. Screw them. I've got half a coffee left and the ability to amuse myself *by* myself. Trust me, people, I do not require the company of others. I've spent plenty of time on my own. Who says a guy needs friends? Maybe some of us were meant to go it alone, like lone wolves. Besides, I have Ramie and a torrid sex life. What do I need other dudes for? To be honest, that Perm guy smelled a little.

So there I am, minding my own beeswax, when the conversation at Larson's table starts to filter into my awareness.

"I'll give you Tilda for that waitress," Alvarez, the black dude, says.

Some tense mumbling ensues, followed by laughter.

To mask my eavesdropping, I start pretend reading the newspaper somebody left on the table.

"Naja's out," Perm, the blond guy, says. "Take her off the board."

They appear to be either trading horses or organizing a girls' sports league, softball perhaps.

"Yeah," Alvarez says. "That number is pushing thirty and looking for a baby daddy."

The others suck their teeth in fear.

Baby daddy?

That doesn't appear to be relevant to the organization of a girls' softball league.

"Yo, punks," Perm says. "You got to put up or shut up. I be carryin' yo asses all summer."

Alvarez shakes his head. "Cuz," he says. "You do realize that you're white. Right?"

I chuckle to myself. I don't like Perm. I don't like his fake yellow hair or his scrawny, freckled arms. I don't like his name either or that pretentious little hat. I think I'm chuckling too loudly, however, because Perm turns around and glares at me.

"Something funny?" he says.

"Huh?" I put the newspaper down and point to their table, where they've got a chart spread out with four names written across the top (Rez, Perm, Larson, and Sasha). About ten girls' names are written down the left-hand side. "Are those softball teams?" I ask.

A tense silence ensues.

Then Alvarez—or "Rez," as I assume he's called by his close friends—laughs sharply. "Softball?"

I look at Larson because we go way back, Larson and me. But Larson has developed an intense fascination with his cuticles.

"You just moved here," Alvarez says. "Right?"

I nod. Alvarez is the only one with any charisma. Plus, he's neither as scrawny nor as scruffy as the other two. I wonder how they all became friends. I point to the chart again. "What is that?"

"It's a chart," Alvarez says. "What does it look like?"

"It looks like a chart," I say. "What's it for?"

"That is strictly for the members to know," Alvarez says.

"Yeah," Perm says. "And I don't see your name here." His glare takes on an edge of pure menace. Sadly for him, it fails to inspire fear. He's too tiny to be threatening. I could fold him in quarters and stuff him in my pocket.

"What's up with your name?" I ask him. "Is it foreign, or are you named after a hair treatment?"

Larson breaks his nervous silence to mutter, "Please don't ask that."

"Lars," Perm says. "I didn't come up with the name. It was bestowed on me."

"Let me tell the story," Alvarez says, all excited.

Perm puts on a show of resisting but ultimately acquiesces. He obviously likes being talked about, and Alvarez, the P. T. Barnum of the gang, likes to talk.

Alvarez pushes his chair back from the table and puts his arm around a vacant chair to take up some space. "So Daryl here," he says, gesturing toward Perm, "goes back with this girl, right?"

"Back where?" I ask.

"To her apartment," he says. "Where do you think?"

Perm points to the name *Alicia* on the board.

"And after the deed is done—" Alvarez says. "You do know what I am referring to by the deed, right?"

"Um." I let my eyes wander to the ceiling. "Are you talking about sexual intercourse?"

"Yeah," Alvarez says. "I didn't know if you were one of those virginal Christian types."

"Do I look like a virginal Christian type?"

"You look like a man who keeps interrupting my story."

"Sorry."

"So Daryl's heading to the door for a speedy exit," he says. "Right?"

Perm purses his lips in distaste. "Worth *one*. But not two."

"Yeah?" Larson says. "So why's she on the board, then?"

"Because some of you losers *like* fat chicks."

"Can I finish this?" Alvarez says.

Everyone quiets down.

Alvarez glances around the room. Whether it's to ensure that no one is listening or that *everyone* is listening, I can't be sure. "So Daryl's looking for a way out that won't totally humiliate this girl, because he's a decent human being, right?"

"I'm a one-man charity," Perm says.

"So this girl. She gets right up in his face and says"—Alvarez puts on a cartoon girl's voice—" 'Daryl, you can't just screw me once and leave. I want more.' "

Larson shakes his head. "No girl has ever said that to me. No girl has ever said anything *like* that to me."

"So Daryl, right?" Alvarez continues. "Friggin' Gandhi over here, says to this chick . . ." Alvarez makes a grand gesture toward Perm.

Perm clears his throat first. "What I said was, 'When I screw a girl, she stays screwed.' "

Alvarez lets rip with a riotous laugh. "How beautiful is that?"

Larson rolls his eyes subtly. "He's been Permascrew ever since."

"Lars, man," Perm says. "You're the one who came up with the name."

Alvarez leans toward me. "I have been in search of opportunities to steal that line ever since, but no girl has ever set me up for it. You see, you need the assist. You basically need a girl to ask for more."

"It's amazing how rarely they do that," Larson says.

There's a pregnant silence as they all stare at me. But I'm not sure what to say, because that is one of the most decrepit stories I've ever heard.

I point to the name *Alicia* on the chart. "Is that the girl?"

The three of them nod.

"And the others?" I say. "Are these all the girls you've gone out with?"

"Gone out with?" Perm says with finger quotes.

"Why is that funny?" I say. "Don't you say that around here?"

"Do they say that in Mayberry?" Perm asks.

"Where's Mayberry?"

The three of them look at each other, then laugh.

Should I know where Mayberry is?

I take a closer look at the chart. Most of the girls have at least two X's in their row. Some have three or four. Perm has the most X's in his column, followed by Alvarez, then Larson, then Sasha, a "member" in absentia apparently. The closer I look, the more ridiculous it seems that I ever thought this matrix represented a girls' softball league.

"Wait a minute," I say. "Are you guys *trading* girlfriends?"

They all exchange nervous glances, then Alvarez shakes his head. "They're not our girlfriends."

"No," Perm says. "They're softball players."

Larson chuckles quietly, obviously eager to curry favor with Perm at my expense. What a prince. I have a sudden desire to beat him senseless, which, on the bright side, is another Novel Sensation.

"But you *are* trading them," I say. "I heard you earlier."

"We're not animals," Perm says. "We don't own these women."

Alvarez points to the name *Kristabel* and says, "Actually, this chick is into that."

"Really?" Larson says.

Perm shakes his head. "Rez, man. She doesn't want to be *owned*. She wants to be humiliated. It's totally different."

Alvarez nods like a dim student who's just had the difference between the Enlightenment and the Renaissance explained to him.

"She *wants* to be humiliated?" I say.

"Why not?" Perm snorts. "Some chicks are into that."

Alvarez looks at Larson. "So are some dudes I know."

"Shut up," Larson says.

"Anyway," Perm says, "if you don't mind, Mayberry, we've got business to attend to." He turns his back to me and takes a pen from his back pocket. "Got another one for you losers, not that you deserve it." He writes the name Melissa K. at the bottom of the list of girls.

"Stats?" Alvarez says.

"Oral?" Perm says. "A minus. However . . ." He cranes his neck over his shoulder to look at me again.

I admit, I'm staring.

"You going to refill our coffees or something, Mayberry?" Perm says.

"Oral A minus?" I say. "What does that mean?"

Alvarez laughs at me. "Man," he says. "You are quite possibly the most annoying person in Williamsburg. Did you not hear me say this is a members-only arrangement?"

"Yeah, but do these girls know you're writing their names in a chart? And trading them like . . . like horses?"

Perm shakes his head. "Any of these girls look like horses to you guys?"

Alvarez shakes his head. "I do not date women who look like horses. Dude, rule number one is you do not bring dog meat to the party."

I stare at Alvarez, bewildered, because I was starting to like him. "Dog meat?" I say.

"Rule number two," he says, taking a sip of his coffee. "Never pass on a bad lay."

"But keep in mind," Perm says, "that one man's trash is another man's treasure."

I stare at Perm for a long time, slowly digesting his words, until he snaps his fingers in my face.

"Are you blacking out or something?" he says.

Perhaps I *am* blacking out, because suddenly it all starts to feel like a dream. A violent dream. In fact, I've never been so consumed with the desire for violence. I envision launching myself like a man missile at Perm's freckled face, then grabbing Larson and Alvarez by the scruffs of the neck and banging their heads together Three Stooges–style.

And I don't know why.

"Man," Alvarez says. "Do you think he's having a seizure?"

Before my desire for violence gets the better of me, I put my coat on and head to the door.

"Yo, Jack," Alvarez says. "We were kind enough to share our life's work with you. Now, I know you'll respect our privacy, right?"

I don't answer. I just slip outside. As I make my way down Bedford Avenue, my whole body bristles with rage. But I'm not even sure what I'm so angry about. After walking a few blocks, I hear someone yell out, "Yo, Jack."

I stop and spot Larson speedwalking toward me. When he catches up to me, he's out of breath. "Dude," he says. "What was that all about?"

"Huh?" I say.

"Back there," he says. "Why'd you get all weird on us?"

"Weird?" I say. "*I'm* weird? You're the one with the girl chart."

"So?" he says.

As I stare into Larson's confused face, it suddenly becomes clear to me why I'm so mad at him and his friends. "How would you like it if a girl put *your* name on a chart?" I ask.

"I don't know," he says. "I probably wouldn't mind, though. Especially if I didn't know about it."

"Oh," I say. "Right. So as long as they don't know about it, it's okay? Yeah. I think that was Gandhi's underlying message. Or was it Jesus? Yeah, I think that's what they call the golden rule, right? Do unto others whatever you want as long as they don't find out."

Larson stares at me with his face all squinty, as if *I* were the one not making sense.

Look, I know I'm not exactly worldly, and I suppose it's possible that skipping high school has left me permanently ignorant about dating and stuff. But for crud's sake, a girl has a right to expect that her name isn't being put on a chart. I mean, come on!

"We're not doing anything against their will," Larson says. "It's just, you know, sometimes things don't work out with a girl, but . . ." His voice trails off, and he shrugs.

"But what?" I say.

Very quietly Larson says, "Just because a girl's no good for you doesn't mean she's no good for your friends."

My stomach turns over. "That's your philosophy?" I say.

"It's not a philosophy," he says.

"No," I say. "You're right. Truth, justice, and the American way is a philosophy. Live and let live is a philosophy. Never bring dog meat to the party? That's not a very good philosophy."

"Jesus," he says. "Do you cry at the opera too?"

"What?"

"I hate to break it to you," he says. "But you sound like a girl."

The next thing I know, Larson is pressed up against a

chain-link fence with my whitened fists balled around the collar of his jacket. The testosterone rush is overpowering, almost erotic.

Larson goes limp, like a kitten that's been picked up by the scruff of its neck. A few feet away, two girls selling used clothes from a blanket on the sidewalk stare at us. I look at Larson dead-on as hot, liquid rage courses through me. He doesn't fight back. He doesn't even try to get away. He just pulls his face as far from mine as possible without actually resisting my grip.

"Larson?" one of the girls says. "Are you okay?"

"Are you going to let go of me?" Larson's voice and demeanor are unnaturally calm, as if being pushed up against a chain-link fence were an everyday occurrence.

I let go, and Larson fixes his jacket. "Hey, Kendra," he says in a lighthearted tone.

The girl nods at him inquisitively. Larson steps a few feet away and gestures for me to join him, which I do.

"Shit, man," he says. "I don't know what your problem is, but it's definitely not in your interest to start spreading this around."

"Spreading what around?" I say too loudly. "The fact that you and your posse have to share girlfriends to avoid ass-drilling each other?"

Kendra looks up from the blanket, where she's just spread out an old skirt.

Larson smiles weakly at her, then looks at me. He's not a fighter. That's obvious. I'm not sure I am either, despite that sudden burst of malfeasance with the chain-link fence. Now that the testosterone rush has dissipated, I'm starting to feel guilty.

"Look," Larson says in a mood of conciliation. "I don't know why you're getting all high-and-mighty. It's not like we're doing anything wrong." His eyes keep flicking back to Kendra and her friend, who are obviously whispering about us while they arrange their sale items on the sidewalk.

"You think they don't talk about us like that?" he says. "You think they don't manipulate us? This is defense, man. They're in control of everything."

"Yeah," I say. "It's a chick's world."

"Like you'd know," he says. "What are you, sixteen?"

"Eighteen," I say. "And actually, I know a couple of things about girls."

"You don't know shit," he says. "Whatever you think you know, that's just Mayberry."

"What the hell is Mayberry?"

"Mayberry is every place that's not New York," he says. "In case you haven't noticed, it's different here. It's not like high school. If you keep thinking it is, they're going to eat you alive." Larson turns around and slouches back down Bedford Avenue.

"Oh yeah?" I say to his retreating back. "Nothing's going to eat me, pal."

The girls selling clothes on the sidewalk look at me and giggle.

"Except for my girlfriend," I say for their benefit. Then I head home.

Alone.

And that is my first morning in New York City.

●

Thankfully, Ramie gets home around four-thirty with thrilling factoids about the history of textiles. I do my best to feign interest. I want to tell her all about my eventful morning, but by the time she finishes talking, we're already taking off each other's clothes. I told you I was a love god.

Around seven o'clock, spent and starving, we pick up a pizza and some ginger ale, then take it to the roof for some alfresco dining Brooklyn-style.

As the sun dips behind the Manhattan skyline, I tell her about the girl-traders and my brief flirtation with violence. I'm a little scared of how she'll react, but keeping secrets from the human mind probe is virtually impossible. Besides, I preface the whole tale by explaining my entirely defensible aim of making new friends.

"They had a chart?" she says. "I have to puke now."

"So I did the right thing?" I say.

Ramie crosses her legs in the little beach chair and has a good, hard think about this. Then she nods. "I'm a pacifist, so normally I would oppose the use of violence, but in this case it was justified because it was targeted and non-malicious."

That sounds like an excellent definition of justifiable violence, but in all honesty, my actions were neither targeted nor non-malicious. I was, at the time, a mindless force of destruction and probably would have strangled a kitten were it at hand.

"Were they trying to recruit you?" she asks.

I shrug. "At first they were all mysterious and secretive

about it. But then I think they were showing off, like they were proud of it."

"Proud of it?" Ramie holds her stomach. "Mal. It reminds me of that time Brandon Dietrick circulated the Least Doable List all over the high school. Poor Stephie LaForge ran out of English class crying. Why are guys like that? Why do they think it's cool to be mean to girls?"

I shake my head. "Beats me."

"Thank God you're not a guy."

"I know," I say. "This one dude, Alvarez, actually referred to girls as dog meat. Wait. What do you mean I'm not a guy?"

"You're *deeply* not a guy," she says.

"How am I not a guy?"

"Duh," she says. "There is nothing guylike about you."

"Excuse me?" I say.

She looks right at me with those dark eyes. "Jack, please. Trust me. You're not a guy."

"Do you mean I'm not a perverted girl-trading jerk, but I'm still, like, a man?"

She looks at me with narrowed eyes.

"Wait a minute," I say. "You have to *think* about this?"

"Jack," she says. "Stop being so conventional. Jeeze."

I take a few breaths to calm down. "Ramie," I say. "I hate to break it to you, but you know that person you've been having sex with since June?"

"Yeah," she says.

"He's a guy."

"No he isn't."

"Well, he's a man. He's a boy at the very least."

She stares at me for a few seconds, then smiles mysteriously. "Sure he is."

"What does that mean? Are you telling me you don't even see me as male?"

She takes a giant swig of ginger ale, then comes over and plops herself in my lap, which almost collapses the beach chair I'm sitting in. "What do you think it means?" she says. "You are a complete original." She kisses me on the forehead. "You would never act like those guys. You *could* never act like them, because you're different." She pulls back and looks at me seriously. "Right?"

I look into her dark brown eyes. Of course I would never act like them. But I'm still a guy. Why do *they* get to define it? Why can't a guy be someone like me?

Ramie wraps her arms around my head and pulls my cheek to her breasts. Before long, I get lost in the moment. It's easy to do when the moment comprises Ramie sliding her hands up the back of my shirt. But the tiny portion of my brain reserved for extraneous non–sex-related thoughts keeps dipping into the darkness of a new and terrifying question.

If I'm not a guy to her, what am I?

september 12

●

Jill

The first thing I notice when I open my eyes is the sound of heavy breathing. The second is the fact that I seem to have grown a third arm. Realizing that neither the arm nor the breathing is my own, I roll over to discover Ramie lying face-down in my bed, her arm slung over me. We're both wearing Jack's boxers.

Mal, why can't they use *her* bed?

I peel myself out from under her arm as sneakily as possible, then tiptoe out and head to the bathroom for a shower.

In the old days, I would begin my first day back by obliterating all memories of Jacktime through my brilliant self-hypnosis regime known as Plan B. Not anymore. I'm trying to reverse all that. So, as the warm water envelops me, I try to relax and let the Jackmemories surface. It's not that I enjoy these memories. Believe me, it was much easier being a cyclical amnesiac. But if I'm going to be a responsible adult who makes important life decisions with both of our interests in mind, I have to make an effort to know my alter ego. I guess you could call this Plan C.

Per usual, only a few dim memories survive the journey from Jacktime to Jilltime: pizza and ginger ale on the roof, sex with Ramie, *more* sex with Ramie.

"Hey, babe!"

The shower curtain whips open, and there is Ramie, topless and yawning ferociously.

"Oh," she says, staring unabashedly. "Sorry. I lost track of time."

"Noticed," I say.

She keeps staring at me, her toes curling against the cold tile floor.

"Ramie?" I say. "Do you mind?"

She cocks her head to the side. "You look great with short hair," she says. "You should ditch the wig."

I run my fingers through my wet hair, which is still only about two inches long.

"No thanks," I say. "Too butch."

Ramie nods, then backs out of the bathroom, but she keeps staring at me. "Hmm," she says.

I yank the shower curtain closed. I don't want to know what she means by "Hmm." With Ramie, it could be anything.

"Yes, Mom, I *love* being a temp secretary. It's deeply fulfilling."

There is a brief pause over the T-Mobile network while Mom scrolls through her database of anti-sarcasm defenses. She's a smart woman. She always calls between 8:35 and 8:49 a.m. because that's when I'm walking from the subway to whatever glass-and-steel tower needs a temp for the day.

"That's a nice bit of snark, young lady," Mom says. "But when are you going to start thinking about college?"

Just to keep her on her toes, I say, "Mom, I'm already gainfully employed typing spreadsheets and answering phones for important people. College is for losers."

"Don't be cynical," she says. "You don't have the cheekbones for it."

"Huh?"

I arrive at the glass-and-steel tower that needs me for the day and look at my reflection in the lobby window. What exactly do cynical cheekbones look like?

"Jill, honey. Listen to me. Can you be serious for a minute? Can you do that?"

"All right." I pull the heavy door open and head into the gaping marble lobby. "I'll be serious. Just, you know, next year."

"Why not next semester?"

"Um . . . let me think about that and get back to you." I find the glassed-in human resources office and go stand outside of it. "I have to go, okay?"

"Honey," she says. "Just don't break my heart by wasting your life. That's all I'm saying."

"I won't."

"Because all it takes is a few bad decisions here and there."

"Mom!" I peel away from the human resources office and hang back by the coffee vendor. "You know, you're really making my Monday a lighthearted affair. I'm not going to pick up the next time you call."

"Yes you will."

She's right. I can't resist speaking to her in the morning. It's a small connection to the old days when we used to chat over breakfast. I hate that she knows this.

"Mom, listen. I'm not wasting my life. I'm trying to figure out how to *live* it. If anyone's wasting his life, it's Jack. All he ever does is eat pizza and have sex with Ramie. Why don't you pester him?"

"Oh God," Mom says. "Please tell me he uses protection."

"Don't worry," I say. "Ramie insists on it." I don't tell my mother about all the condom wrappers I find around the apartment, because I doubt she'd appreciate the visuals.

"Look," I say. "My real job, for the time being anyway, is finding a way to coexist with Jack in a way that doesn't drive us both nuts. Once I iron out those details, I will deeply go to college. I promise."

Mom takes her time sighing meaningfully, just to reiterate how concerned she is. Then she says, "I love you, honey," in that surprisingly soft tone of voice she occasionally adopts. I swear she hauls that out just to keep me hooked.

It works too.

When we hang up, I get my assignment sheet and temporary ID from a woman in HR, then head for the elevator, happy to disappear into the anonymity of the crowd.

All temp assignments are basically the same. You sit at a wood veneer desk outside a bank of window offices, answer the phone once in a while, and wait for people to give you stuff to enter into a computer. That's it. Temping does *not* provide a window into a variety of fascinating careers, nor does it allow you to network with interesting and useful people. I admit, in my naïveté, I was hoping for both.

What temping does provide, besides cold, hard cash, is a lot of downtime. The phone rings only so often and there are only so many spreadsheets to type up. The rest of the time I spend Net surfing and waiting around for texts from the increasingly mysterious Tommy Knutson.

Tommy doesn't e-mail. He doesn't phone. He doesn't send care packages or mini-bagel baskets. All he does is text. These are occasionally provocative and usually cryptic.

Example:

Arkansas midnite. 2 many stars. Where R U?

How can there be too many stars? And where does he *think* I am? I'm in New York, where he left me.

Once he texted:

remember that wednesday?

When I texted back:

which wednesday?

He waited two whole days, then texted:

still no cat, I hope.

Tommy has never texted:

jill, I luv u more than words can say.

(re)cycler

Or

I can't believe I'm driving so far away from u when all I want is 2 come bck 2 Bkln and make luv 2 U.

To be fair, neither have I.

I'm not sure it would jibe with the Play It by Ear guidelines. Trying to figure out what the Play It by Ear guidelines are is another way I kill time as a temp.

Ramie thinks I should cease all Tommy-related thought because it's making me angsty. But given the soul-destroying tedium of my job, I think angst is my only bulwark against cynicism, for which I lack the proper cheekbones.

Do you see the bind I'm in?

So one Saturday morning I'm walking home from the supermarket with some Grape Nuts and milk while pondering how I might go about *not* angst-ing out over Tommy Knutson. There's a crisp autumn chill in the air, a sensation that always brings to mind new beginnings—the first day of school, a new wardrobe, etc. But this is Brooklyn, New York, not Winterhead, Massachusetts, so there's a delicious sense of unfamiliarity mixed in too. The biggest difference is the huge number of people walking around. You almost never see people walking in Winterhead. Here, it's humanity as far as the eye can see.

Inherent in New York's sheer volume of humanity is its impressive quantity of cute guys. They're everywhere! In fact, there's one across the street sneaking glances at me while he's waiting for the light to change. With his sly smile and his broad shoulders, he could easily distract me from Tommy Knutson for a few hours. Who knows, maybe even for a few weeks.

To screw up my courage, I tell myself that smiling at cute strangers is almost certainly within the Play It by Ear guidelines and that Tommy Knutson is probably smiling at people *all the time*. Not to mention, being bi, he has twice the smiling options I have.

When the light changes and the cute guy and I head toward each other to cross the street, I want so much to smile at him. But as soon as he looks at me, I avert my eyes and rush to the other side.

As I stand on the corner and watch him walk away, I feel defeated and more than ever like a little girl. A little girl who's not over Tommy Knutson yet. I don't want to be this way. I want to be the kind of girl who's so over Tommy Knutson that smiling at cute strangers is a piece of cake. But I've only ever smiled at boys who were vetted by the Winterhead public school system. I'm not sure *how* to smile at strangers. I was explicitly told not to do that.

I shuffle homeward with my eyes on the sidewalk, cursing my stupid upbringing for making me overly cautious. At times like these, I suspect that I'm not ready for life on my own in the big city.

When I get to my building, there is a young woman in her twenties sitting on my stoop, hunched over and nervously biting her fingernails. She has pale skin, jet-black hair, and she's dressed in a bright blue trench coat with the collar up. I can't tell if she's hiding from someone or spying on someone, but she's definitely blocking my way.

"Excuse me," I say.

"Oh good," she says. "Stand there." She grabs my legs and moves me into position right in front of her. Then, using my body as a shield, she peers out at a black town car inching slowly across the intersection half a block away.

"Can you *believe* this guy?" she mutters into my hip bone. "Do you have a pen?"

"Um, no."

She squints at the town car. "Communicar. Number four seventy-eight. Remember that, okay? God, what a stalker." She looks up at me. "Do you live here?"

I nod.

She looks me up and down. "How old are you?"

"Eighteen," I say. "Do *you* live here?"

She waves her hand to shut me up, then pulls me close and practically buries her face in my stomach. "Don't move."

I sneak a peek over my shoulder and spot the town car heading slowly toward us, its windows black.

"Oh, he did not!" She takes a deep breath, then stands up and pushes past me. "Hey *Kevin!*" She sneers the name. "Why don't you grow a pair and get out of the car!"

The car stops.

"Oh no." She turns around, pushes past me up the stairs, and fumbles her key into the lock. "Oh crap oh crap oh crap," she says. Her keys clatter down the fake marble steps.

The rear door of the town car opens a crack, revealing the pant leg of a gray suit.

"Who is that?" I say. I head up the stairs with my own key and open the door for her.

She picks up her keys, then grabs my hand and drags me up to the second floor. "Be my witness," she says. She gets her door open with a shove, then drags me inside and over to the window.

Down below, the car door opens all the way, and a chubby, balding guy gets out wearing a gray suit. It's the same gray suit that all business guys wear.

"That's who you're afraid of?" I say.

He looks like George Costanza.

She hides next to the window and peers out through the curtain.

The guy stands outside of the car looking up at the second-floor window for a few seconds. He sighs, then gets back into the car, and it drives off.

The girl sighs in relief. "Okay," she says. "You saw that. So if anything happens to me, that's the guy. Kevin Jelivek. J-e-l-i-v-e-k. I trust you can spell Kevin on your own." She heads to the kitchen.

"What did he do?" I say.

"Are you kidding? Thirty-six texts in twenty-four hours. That's what."

"He looked old," I say.

She nods. "Thirty-two. Rich. Very liquid. I mean, I appreciate all the sushi, but I'm bored now." She opens a can of diet

cream soda and pours it into a jam jar with some ice. "I'm Natalie, by the way. When did you move in? Are you a trustafarian? Please say no. I've already met my quota of people I need
to hate for the week."

"What's a trustafarian?"

She takes a sip, then scrunches up her face as she looks at me.

Her apartment is laid out exactly like ours, with similar
scavenged furniture. But there are a few framed photos and
paintings on the wall and some cute pillows on the sofa. She's
made it into a home. She takes her bright blue trench coat off,
revealing a double-breasted tartan jacket.

"Wow," I say. "Is that Vivienne Westwood?"

She cocks her head at me. "Yeah, right," she says. "Like I can
afford that."

"It looks like Vivienne Westwood. Where'd you get it?"

She smiles and has another sip.

The next thing I know, Natalie is guiding me around the perils
and pitfalls of Williamsburg's abundant vintage clothing stores
while regaling me with stories from her adventure-filled life.
Vital stats? She's twenty-three, recently graduated from New
York University, and eking out a living editing a brand-new
magazine called *Life Before the Apocalypse,* which is financed by
a bunch of "know-nothing wankers."

(A trustafarian, by the way, is an "obnoxious rich kid living
in an expensive apartment purchased by Mummy and Daddy."
Everyone hates them, except in the summer, when they tend to
have beach houses with spare bedrooms.)

Natalie is *not* afraid of smiling at cute strangers and, in fact, flirts with almost every guy she sees, because "you never know."

While we're heading down North Eleventh Street, Natalie pulls me to a screeching stop and forces me to look at my reflection in a drugstore window.

"Why are you so hostile to color?" she asks.

"Well, my friend Ramie says that monochromatic is really big right now and that mixing shades of gray is—"

"Your friend Ramie doesn't know what she's talking about. Look. You blend right into the buildings. And these aren't pretty buildings."

I have to admit, next to Natalie in her bright blue coat I do look drab.

"You're young," she says. "You have that going for you. But do you have any idea how vastly we outnumber them in this city? You have to do more than look like jailbait. Come on."

She takes my hand and leads me away. I have to admit it's pretty funny that Natalie just assumes my only goal in life is to pick up guys. I guess she assumes it's every girl's goal. It's not, of course (well, it's not my *only* goal), but I don't mind going along for the ride. I'm here to learn, after all. I may as well learn from her.

Natalie takes me to a big vintage store called Beacon's Closet. Once inside, she scours the racks like a pro, choosing only the brightest clothes. After making me try on half the store, we decide (or I should say *she* decides) on one pouffy-shouldered red satin blouse plus one slouchy green leather bag.

Total cost: seventeen dollars.

Approving nod from new shopping buddy: priceless.

Natalie makes me wear the blouse out the door and stuff my gray canvas backpack into the green bag as we make our way toward Bedford Avenue.

"Twice as doable already," she says. "Look." She yanks me to a stop in front of that drugstore window again.

"Red and green, though?" I say. "It's not too Christmassy?"

"Possibly," she says. "Still, at least I can see you now. Before, you were like a lamppost or a piece of litter on the sidewalk. I was like, hello, wasn't I walking down the street with someone? Oh yeah, there she is."

We get lunch at Dexter's, where Natalie is able to convince Joel the bartender to serve me a beer despite the fact that he knows I'm underage. At Natalie's insistence, I put on some of her bright red lipstick, using the back of a spoon for a mirror, while she explains the difference between a slut and a vamp.

Slut: promiscuous girl with low self-esteem who uses sex to win men's approval.

Vamp: promiscuous *woman* who doesn't give a shit.

Guess which one Natalie is.

While she's talking, I can't help but notice this hot guy over at the bar who keeps looking at me.

Without even glancing back, Natalie says, "Describe him."

"Tall," I say. "Thin. Dark hair."

Natalie nods. "Sort of distant-looking? Like he's either philosophical or lost?"

"Exactly."

"Sounds like Ian." She uses her own spoon to sneak a look at him. "Yup. Ian. You like them skinny, huh?"

I shrug. I'm a little tipsy from the beer, so I'm tending to like everything. I'm hoping the beer will pickle my senses just enough to embolden me to smile at him, a move that is not only in the Play It by Ear Guidebook I'm mentally composing, but also an absolute requirement for an aspiring vamp.

"Do you know him?" I ask.

She takes a sip of her beer. "I know his friends. Total players. Do not ask me how I know this."

Natalie snaps her fingers at the bartender. "Barkeep," she says. "Another round."

Joel shakes his head.

"Oh, don't be such a fascist," she says. "I'm developing a future client."

Joel brings over one beer for Natalie. "I'm trying to keep my job," he says. "Sorry, Jill. It's not me. It's the law."

"It's okay," I say. Then I whisper, "I'm already drunk."

"That's excellent." He glares at Natalie, then walks back to the bar.

"Fine," she says. "Be an agent of the police state. Whatever." She takes a sip, then pushes her beer toward me.

"I shouldn't," I say.

Just then I notice that Ian, the cute guy at the bar, is walking toward us. "Here he comes," I whisper. "Quick, what do I do?"

"Use a condom," she says. Then, smooth as silk, she kicks a vacant chair out from under the lip of our table. "Ian, right?"

she says. "Meet Jill." She stands up and heads to the ladies' room. "Do *not* talk about me when I'm gone."

Ian watches her go, then sits at our table without saying anything. There's something vaguely familiar about him, but that's probably because he has what I've come to regard as the official Williamsburg guy look, which consists of disheveled hair, a few days' growth of beard, and studiously sloppy but tight-fitting clothes. In my head, I start psyching myself up to smile at him, but he doesn't smile at me right away, so I decide to hold it in reserve.

"How old are you?" he says.

I almost lie and tell him I'm twenty-three, like Natalie, but I'm not drunk enough to believe I can pull that off.

"Eight—" I freeze. "Nineteen?" I say.

"Eight-nineteen?" he says. "That's not an age. That's a time."

"I meant . . ." I pause, incapable of deciding whether to go with the lie or the truth. Is there any advantage to being nineteen over eighteen? If I lie about it now, will I have to keep lying for the rest of my life?

"Eighteen," I say. "I meant eighteen. How old are you?"

"Twenty-four," he says.

His eyes flick up to mine for a moment, then dart away.

It's weird, but it almost seems like I'm making *him* nervous.

"Have we met before?" he asks.

I shake my head. "Maybe in a dream," I say.

He looks away and laughs. Then, a few seconds later, he looks right at me and smiles. *This is it,* I think. *I'm either a grown woman or a little girl. What's it going to be?* It takes all of my strength to resist the temptation to look down nervously and pick at my fingers. But somehow (perhaps it's the beer) I manage to look right into his eyes and smile back.

That's me, ladies and gentlemen. Uber-sophisticated New York City vamp wearing vintage clothes and bright red lipstick, drinking beer, and smiling brazenly at a cute stranger.

What began as lunch stretches out to seven o'clock, during which time Ramie joins us, along with Ian's friend Sasha, a guy who's kind of chubby but nice in a nerdy way. Natalie has seen the bottom of four bottles of beer and is telling us about how her magazine is going to "change everything."

Ian thinks I'm hot. I can tell by the way he keeps looking at me. At one point, while Natalie's telling us about how one of her investors broke up with her *while* she was going down on him, Ian leans over and touches his lips to my ear.

"Do you want to get out of here?" he whispers.

I pull away from him in shock. Actually, I'm in double shock, both by Ian's forwardness and by Natalie's disgusting story. I can almost feel my fledgling status as an uber-sophisticated New York City vamp evaporating into thin air. Thankfully, Ramie notices my situation and leans across the table to rub at my eyebrow with her thumb.

"Makeup emergency," she says. "Girls' room. Now."

We leave Natalie and the boys behind and head to the bathroom. Once inside, Ramie shuts the door and makes sure we have the place to ourselves.

"Mal," Ramie says. "Natalie sure has some stories. Do you think they're all true?"

"Why would she lie?" I ask.

I stumble into a stall to pee.

"All right," she says. "Get it out of your system."

"I am."

"Not that," she says. "I mean reasons for you not to sleep with that guy."

"Ramie!" I say. "I'm not going to get drunk and sleep with the first guy who comes along."

She peers over the top of the door. "He *is* non-ugly," she says. "And he's not the first one to come along. Remember that guy in the park?"

"He smelled like onions."

"All guys smell like onions sometimes. Stop making excuses."

"Do you mind?"

She sighs and pulls herself away.

What I don't tell Ramie is that it feels *wrong* to flirt with Ian. It feels like cheating. But I know this is the result of temporary brain damage from my Tommy Knutson love hangover, so I choose to repress it. Don't knock repression. It's a powerful tool.

When I join Ramie at the mirror, I cannot believe how awful Natalie's bright red lipstick looks.

"Rames! Why didn't you tell me?" I grab a paper towel and start wiping it off. "I look like the mouth that ate Brooklyn."

"I thought that's what you were going for." She hands me a

small tub of Vaseline from her purse, followed by a tube of pink lip gloss. "Strawberry," she says. "So your kisses will taste good."

"I haven't decided if I'm going to kiss him yet." I put her lip gloss on, then look in the mirror. "I do like him. But don't you think there's something, I don't know, kind of scary about him?"

"What?" she says. "Like the fact that he's *twenty-four*?"

"Yeah," I say. "I've never dated in the twenties. That's like skipping grades."

"I know!" She nods excitedly. "Hey, Sasha's kind of cute, right?"

"Ramie."

"What? I can notice a guy is cute. Jill, please tell me you're not spying on me for Jack."

"Dude," I say. "Jack spies on *me*."

"Well, I wasn't planning on doing anything," she says. "I'm just being a good wingman."

"Dutifully remembered," I say.

"I can't believe you're going to narc me out to Jack!"

"Ramie," I say. "Do you not understand the mechanics of our situation?"

"Right," she says. "But just so we're clear, I am strictly on wingman duty."

"And I am deeply going to remember that sentence so Jack won't suspect you of cheating. Can we bring it back to *me* now?"

"Sorry."

"Okay," I say. "Let's say I do want to kiss Ian. How do I make that happen without looking slutty? Vampy is fine."

"Vampy?"

"Yeah."

"Hmm." Ramie leans against the sink with me and has a think.

We say nothing for a while, as our brains churn. Oddly, I find myself wondering what Jack would do in this situation. Then I realize Jack would have stolen Ian's wallet by now to get his address. Then he'd stake out his bedroom window from a tree.

"You know what?" I say. "Screw it. I'm just going to kiss him." I head to the door.

"Good plan." She grabs her purse and follows me.

Once outside the bathroom, I notice that Natalie has gone, but two more guys have joined Ian and Sasha. I pull Ramie back. "You think those are the guys Natalie warned me about? You know, the total players?"

"Unknown," she says. "The black guy's cute, though. Is that racist?"

"Possibly," I say. "Can girls be players?"

"Of course," she says.

I head toward them, but Ramie pulls me back and shoves her face in my neck.

"Can you believe we're actually hanging out in a bar in New York?" she says. "With guys in their twenties?"

"I know!" I say. "Okay, stop being giddy."

"Right. Right."

Ramie puts on a blank expression, then joins me as we head back to our table, cool as cukes. By the time we get there, the two other guys have made themselves scarce.

"This place is starting to suck," Ian says.

I glance around. Dexter's has filled up with people I would not describe as sucking. In fact, I would describe them as the height of cool.

"Yeah," I say. "Maybe we should go."

Ramie gives me the stink eye.

"I mean maybe we should all go together," I say. "We could . . . get some beer and . . . go up to our roof?"

Ian and Sasha shoot each other glances, but what those glances communicate I can't decipher.

Fifteen minutes later I'm standing at the ledge of my roof looking down at one of our neighbors who's peeing against a tree while his dog does the same thing.

"That doesn't seem very neighborly," I say.

When I look up, I notice that Ramie and Sasha have wandered to the other side of the roof, leaving only Ian, who removes a beer from the six-pack.

I do not need a beer. I'm still buzzed from the early one, plus all the sips Natalie snuck me. I take the beer from Ian and vow to pretend drink it. That was my best trick at parties in high school—not that I went to many.

"So," I say. "Who were those two guys at the bar?"

"Just friends," he says. "Natalie knows them."

"How?"

"She dated them."

"Oh," I say. "Both of them?"

He nods. "Yeah. At the same time, actually."

"At the same time?" I say.

He nods.

"Oh," I say. "That's . . ." I almost say *interesting,* but that is something my mother would say, and I am not going to start quoting Helen McTeague. Instead, I leave the sentence unfinished.

Ian keeps his eyes glued to mine as he drinks his beer. "It didn't last long," he says.

I nod. I don't want to give him the impression that I'm scandalized. Perhaps dating two guys at once is a normal, everyday occurrence here. It's funny because before I met Natalie, I would have placed such behavior squarely in the slut column. I guess it belongs in the vamp column, however, because Natalie did it. Live and learn.

"You're not drinking your beer," Ian says.

I take a pretend sip.

After looking at me for a deliciously agonizing four Mississippis, he brushes my arm with the tips of his fingers. "You're really pretty," he says.

I laugh nervously. Ian just keeps looking at me like he means business. I'm able to hold his gaze for a few seconds, but eventually my attention is drawn to the other side of the roof, where Ramie is fake laughing at something Sasha has said. In fact, she's openly flirting. Why would she do that? Surely her wingman duties were satisfied once we arrived on the roof.

Shouldn't she be fake yawning by now? She shouldn't be chatting Sasha up and infusing him with false hopes.

They are false hopes, right?

Soft lips touch my cheek. I'm so startled, I almost fall over.

Ian catches me by the elbow. "Are you all right?" he says.

"Sorry," I say. "I'm a little drunk."

He brings his face close to mine. "I won't tell your parents," he whispers.

"Good," I whisper back. "They're three states away."

I put my bottle on the ledge of the roof. Ian puts his down too, then steps closer. We have already sped from the smiling-at-each-other phase to the looking-at-each-other-seriously phase, and now I sense the rapidly approaching kissing phase. It's all moving so quickly. Just this morning I was unable to smile at strangers.

Ian takes my hand and leans forward slowly. But just before our lips connect, a high-pitched sound rips through the air from the cell phone in my pocket.

It's a text alert.

Only two people text me, and one of them is brazenly flirting on the other side of the roof.

"Do you have to get that?" Ian asks.

I shake my head. Of course I don't *have* to get it. It'll just be Tommy Knutson with another torturously vague text-haiku. Why would I answer *that*?

Politeness alone dictates that I pay more attention to the tall, sleek stranger bearing down on me than to the vague, coded signals casually lobbed by Mr. Play It by Ear. Mr. Play It by Ear is not on my rooftop. He's somewhere west of here, quite possibly (you can't rule it out) screwing his way to San Francisco. For all I know, that's what Play It by Ear means. At any rate, I'm sure it's not in the Play It by Ear Guidebook to spoil the moment with your current crush to retrieve a text from a guy who is not even for definitely sure being faithful to you; who is, when you stop to think about it, breaking your heart in slow motion.

Or am I breaking his?

Ian touches the ends of my wig very gently. Quickly, in the amount of time it takes to screw up my courage, I convince myself that Play It by Ear means whatever I decide it means. Then I do what any uber-sophisticated New York City vamp would do. I stand on my tippy-toes and kiss Ian on the lips. He wraps his arms around me, and before I know it, he's pushed me up against the four-foot ledge of the roof. Our mouths are locked, but my eyes are open. I can see Ramie and Sasha on the other side watching us. Ramie takes Sasha's hand and leads him out of view. I want to know where she's going, but I have other things fighting for my attention.

"Can I stay here tonight?" Ian asks.

I pull back. "What?"

Instead of answering, he kisses me again.

Surely I can't let Ian spend the night so soon in our relationship. Such an act would fall squarely in the slut column, wouldn't it?

On the other hand, I love the way his body feels pressed up against mine.

When my cell phone beeps again, Ian slides his hand into my thigh pocket and grabs it. "You sure you don't want to get that?"

I shake my head.

He turns it off. Then he smiles at me as he puts it back in my pocket. It's a mischievous smile, full of lusty intent.

I do like that about him. It's strange. It's *novel*. It's a completely novel sensation.

And isn't this precisely the kind of new experience that will change me from a girl to a woman? The kind of woman who stands on her rooftop kissing total strangers who are unvetted by the Winterhead public school system? Twelve months of this, and I will be unrecognizable indeed.

But in a good way, I promise.

october 4

●

Jack

The ceramic poodle is grinning at me in double vision and my mouth tastes like something died in it. When I sit up in bed, the room spins. I throw the covers off and lean over the side of the bed with my head in my hands. That's when I realize I'm naked. Jill *never* sleeps naked. Sure, she ditched the lace thongs a while ago—after much complaining from *moi*, re: battered testicles—but these days she usually wears these goofy Tinker Bell pajamas. They're too small for me, but they're made of this soft, stretchy fabric that actually feels nice.

Something's wrong today. Correction: *everything's* wrong. Normally when I wake up, my brain is flooded with sharp, crispy Jillmemories, usually of boring things. This morning I have nothing but cotton between my ears. What did she *do* last night?

The cell phone beeps from across the room and I stalk over to retrieve it, tripping over Jill's last outfit, which lies in a heap on the floor. There's a message from the ever-mysterious TK.

I'm about to retrieve it when I realize that this strange sensation of dizziness and mind cotton is a hangover.

Jill got drunk yesterday!

I take a deep breath and try to dig out more details from Jill-time, but everything's murky. I can picture Dexter's, Ramie, some pretty girl with black hair, a dude named Ian.

Wait a minute. I know that dude. His name's not Ian. It's—

Holy crap! Jill made out with Larson last night. Yes, Larson. Ian Larson. That scrawny linguist who trades girls. He *kissed* us. With tongues!

I storm into the bathroom and brush my teeth so hard it might strip the enamel. Good. I don't want tooth enamel that's been tainted by Ian Larson. What could Jill have been thinking? Could she not *infer* his obvious "malness"? Did he not exude an aroma of pure evil? A scent of sulfur and Altoids?

I throw on a towel and barge into Ramie's empty room. To cleanse the residue of Larson, I dive onto Ramie's unmade bed and rub her pillow all over me. It smells just like her, musty and coconutty. Her black panties hang from a knob on a dresser drawer, and I'm sorry to report that I do not resist the temptation to press them to my face. I don't even hesitate. I lie smothered in Ramie's luscious, purifying aroma, my body responding in exactly the way you'd expect. But when I reach for the old Viking to erase the atrocity of last night with a quick, cleansing wank, more Jillmemories surface.

Strawberry-flavored lip gloss.

The rooftop.

Larson and Jill pawing at each other on one side while, on

the other side, Ramie giddily fake laughs with some chubby guy named *Sasha.*

But Sasha was the fourth name on that chart, which means . . .

Ramie and Jill were double-teamed by girl-traders!

The Viking deflates.

Squeezing my eyes closed, I stay focused on the ever-sharpening memories of last night as Jill's feelings course through me like bad clams. There's guilt for "cheating" on Knutson, plus lust, *actual lust,* for Larson.

But here's the worst part: despite getting all sexed up over Larson's exploration of her gums with his tongue, Jill's attention kept wandering to the other side of the roof, where Ramie was flirting with Sasha. I can see the whole thing clearly now, just as Jill saw it. Sasha's eyes were all over Ramie. And Ramie knew it. She ate it up!

But it gets worse. While Larson pressed Jill to the roof's ledge for a decisive feel-up, Jill peered around the side of his head to watch Ramie take Sasha's hand and lead him away!

Did Jill then throw Mr. Wandering Hands over the roof to follow Ramie downstairs? Did she make any effort whatsoever to discern precisely where Ramie took this complete and utter stranger?

No. She was too busy making out with that skeleton. Larson got his hands all the way up her shirt with an attempt on the clasp of her bra before Jill even wondered where Ramie went.

Some friend.

I rush forward through Jilltime. She and Larson groped and

grabbed at each other on the roof for a while before Jill, re-membering the date and the likelihood of a middle-of-the-night sex change, urged him downstairs and out the door. Then, in a drunken stupor, she stumbled to Ramie's room, put her ear to the door, and, hearing nothing, clomped off to her room, ripped off her clothes, and passed out.

I replay the moment she put her ear to Ramie's door. Absolute silence. No. Some traffic outside. A siren. People yelling on the sidewalk. But from within, nothing.

I sit up on Ramie's bed and do a quick calculation. Approximately twenty minutes passed between Ramie's leading Sasha away by the hand (by the hand!) and Jill's putting her ear to Ramie's door. Theoretically, it's possible that Ramie screwed the guy, then fell asleep. He could have woken up at any point in the night and snuck out.

Wait a minute. I don't even know if Ramie slept here last night.

I bolt off the bed and rummage through all the clothes on Ramie's bedroom floor. A black sweater, pale blue corduroy jeans, which she was wearing last night. That means either she slept here or she slunk back in the early morning hours to change before school.

I run into my room, grab Jill's cell phone, and call her. She doesn't answer. She's probably in class. I text her the following:

Call me. Urgent.

I drop to my bed and stare at the phone, which does not ring. Ramie turns either the ringer or the phone off when she's in class, so it could be minutes or hours before she gets my text.

In all honesty, I cannot rule out the possibility that Ramie had sex with Sasha last night. She was drunk, just like Jill. She was clearly enjoying Sasha's attentions. Earlier in the evening, now that I remember it, she told Jill he was "cute."

Cute! Since when is a fat, bearded scumhole cute?

I have to lie down. I take a few deep breaths and try to stay calm. I don't *know* that Ramie slept with Sasha. There could be a perfectly innocent explanation for everything. Well, not *perfectly* innocent. Jill and Ramie did invite them to the roof. Why would they do that?

It occurs to me just then that in a moment of pitiful wrong-headedness, I sought out Larson's companionship too. Not only did I ask if I could join him at Dexter's, I took the mortifying further step of hoping (it makes me sick now) that he and his degenerate friends would *like* me.

What a tool I am.

Sitting up with a renewed sense of purpose, I throw on some clothes. Jill did not leave me a neat little envelope of cash this time, because she was too wasted to think of anyone but her own whoring self. I know her money and MetroCard are in her giant green bag, so I grab that and storm out the door.

It's cold and gray, and I am not wearing my coat, just jeans and a blue sweater. Still, I walk so briskly through the gloomy streets of Brooklyn that I'm sweating by the time I get to Bedford Avenue. Jill's bag keeps banging into my ankles, so I throw it over my shoulder and keep walking. When I catch my reflection in a store window, however, I stop short. I look like a girl. I try to sling the bag across my chest, messenger-style, but the strap is so short I can only just squeeze my head through. Now it dangles like a giant green tumor from my armpit. I try to squeeze back out of it, but all I manage to do is spin around in a frustrated circle.

"Are you all right?" A guy with a canvas backpack neatly mounted *where it belongs* stops and stares. "Do you need some help?" he says.

"It's eating me," I say.

He looks nervous, a reluctant Samaritan for sure. "Maybe if you . . ." He tries to lift the bag over my head, but this nearly dislocates my shoulder.

"You know what?" I say. With a great tug, I move the bag to my back. The strap presses against my windpipe, but I manage to slide it down before suffocating. "I'm cool," I say. "Thanks."

He nods and walks off.

I check my reflection in the store window. From the front it looks like I'm wearing a green leather gun holster, which I can live with. From the side I am being humped by a turtle. But you know what? I don't have time for this. I peel myself away and rush down Bedford Avenue toward the L train.

When I get to the subway entrance, I dig the cell phone from my front pocket and call Ramie again. She doesn't answer. I think about leaving a voice mail, but I'm so scared and angry about what she might have done that I can barely breathe.

(re)cycler

There's a good chance she got my first text but assumed it was only Jill asking where the tampons are or something else unconvincingly "urgent." I decide to text her something she won't ignore. I text:

Did u screw him?

I remain at the subway entrance while people enter and exit, the fear growing with every second. But no matter how deeply I excavate Jill's memories, I cannot find Ramie in those crucial twenty minutes.

Eventually the cell phone chirps at me. My stomach flips over as I retrieve Ramie's text, which is:

??????

What kind of a reply is that? With furious speed I type:

Sasga did u scrdw him

I don't bother correcting my mistakes. I just hit send.
An agonizing three minutes later she texts back:

Jill?

I respond with:

Jack did u screw him?

The following ensues:

Ramie: who?
Me: Sasha

Ramie: R u nuts?

Me: Why dont u answer

Ramie: Coz ur crazy

Me: Thats not answer!

Ramie: Spy much

Me: ANSWER ME!!!!

Ramie: This conv is over

Me: Just answer!

Ramie does not respond after that. I stand there for five minutes stabbing at my cell phone like a deranged robot. All to no avail.

I'm about to head into the subway when I spot Alvarez across the street. I call out his name, but he doesn't hear me. I rush right into the traffic, causing a car to screech to a halt; then I chase Alvarez for half a block while calling out his name. Eventually he stops, looks around, then peels an earbud from one ear. I run right up to him and grab his shoulder.

He shudders. "Jesus, man!"

"Do you know where Sasha is?" I say. "I need to talk to him. I need to talk to him right now."

Alvarez fumbles with his iPod, then slowly, methodically removes the other earbud. "Why?" he says.

Alvarez is one of them. It may as well have been him possibly (probably?) having sex with Ramie last night. "Just . . ." My hands ball into fists at my side. "I need to know where he is. That's all."

"I haven't seen him." He puts his earbuds back in and walks away.

I rush in front of him and grab his arm.

He rips it away. "Dude!" He looks right through me with eyes full of menace. He's about two inches taller than I am, and something tells me he wouldn't shy from a fight the way Larson did. He leans to the side to have a look at the bag protruding from my back. "Nice purse," he says.

"Look." I back up a tad. "There's a chance—and I really hope I'm wrong about this—but there's a chance that Sasha might have . . ." I swallow and try to fight back the dizzying effects of panic.

"He might have what?" Alvarez says.

I take a deep, cold breath. "He might have had sex with my girlfriend," I say.

Now Alvarez backs up. "Whoa," he says. "Sasha?" He shakes his head doubtfully. "She a Velma?"

"A what?"

"An un-Daphne?" he says. "You know, fachita bowwow?"

"What's that? What do you . . . what do those words mean?"

"Is she *ugly*?" he says.

"No."

Alvarez shakes his head. "It's doubtful, then. Sasha's strictly on dog patrol."

Dog patrol?

So that's why they have a rule against bringing dog meat to the party. Ramie flirted (at least) with a fat loser who gravitates to—or, perhaps, only qualifies for—ugly girls. It's awful on so many different levels.

"Man," Alvarez says. "You need a bitchectomy or something.

This girl is obviously twisting your head up. You see, you can't allow that. You let a girl into your head, she'll infect it like a virus until your brain is all demented."

I look at him, confused.

"Am I talking too fast?" he says. "Listen, buddy—"

"I'm not your buddy."

"Ooh, that was frosty." Alvarez mock shivers. "Have you asked your *girlfriend* if she diddled Sasha?"

I nod.

"Well, what did she say?"

"She said I'm nuts."

Alvarez shrugs evasively. "Sounds like a smart girl. Man, you need to chillax. All that anger's gonna give you acne." He walks off again.

"Alvarez?"

He stops and faces me, clearly irritated at my continued existence in his visual range.

"What about Larson?" I say. "Have you seen him?"

"Why? Did your girl do him too? She into threesomes?"

My jaw tenses. "No," I say through clenched teeth.

Alvarez smiles darkly and looks at the pavement. "You got some serious energy emanating off you."

"Yeah, I know," I say. "Larson made out with a girl last night. A girl named Jill."

"Uh-huh." Alvarez squints. "Brown hair, kind of innocent-looking? Hangs with that skinny fox with the big tits?"

My hands ball into fists again. "Yes," I say. "Her name's Jill, and the skinny fox is my girlfriend."

Alvarez presses his lips together and nods in admiration.

"I need you to tell Larson and Sasha something for me, okay?" I say.

He nods.

"You tell them that both of those girls are off-limits."

Alvarez's eyes drift to something behind me. Turning around, I spot Permascrew and Larson about half a block away. I sprint for them, but Larson turns and runs. Permascrew stands still, but as I run past him to get at Larson, he grabs my arm.

"What's up?" he says. Then, at Larson's retreating back, he yells, "Yo, Larson!"

Larson looks over his shoulder but keeps running. I rip my arm out of Perm's grip. He's stronger than he looks.

I stick my finger right in Perm's face. "Those girls?" I say. "They are off-limits to you."

Alvarez inches toward us and peers around the corner, where Larson disappears behind a building.

"What girls?" Perm says.

"Yeah," Alvarez says. "What's with the other one? Why's she off-limits?"

"Who are these girls we're talking about?" Perm says.

"Jill McTeague," I say. "And Ramie Boulieaux."

Alvarez leans into Permascrew and whispers something.

Permascrew's face brightens with recognition. "That skinny chick?" he says. "She's your girlfriend?" Perm looks me up and down.

"Off-limits," I say. "Both of them."

"Dude," Alvarez says. "I get that you don't want to be

sharing your chick and all, but you can't just declare the other one off-limits. What is she, your sister or something?"

"Yeah," I say. "She's my sister."

"Well," Perm says. "From what I hear, your sister invited Larson back to her place, so maybe you ought to be having this conversation with her."

"Don't worry," I say. "I will." I walk away and head for the subway.

"You know you have a girl's pocketbook stuck to your back!" Alvarez shouts.

"I know what's stuck to me!" I shout back.

As the L train speeds under the East River on its way to Manhattan, I distract myself from the stomach-churning horror of Ramie's possible (probable?) indiscretion by conjuring fanciful images of Sasha's face as I punch him into a coma. This gives me no pleasure. Yes, it's a Novel Sensation, I suppose, but I'd gladly relinquish it. I've felt despair before. You could say I'm a connoisseur of despair. But this sharp ache is something entirely new.

If it's true, if Ramie has done what I fear she has done, I'll never recover. How could I? It's obscene. An affront to the logic of the universe itself. Ramie belongs to *me*. Surely she knows this. It's inevitable, ordained, almost biological. And I belong to her. That's just how it is. And how it must always be.

After a switch to the 1 train, I arrive at the FIT campus. I have no idea where to find Ramie, so I park myself in a diner and send her one text every five minutes while consuming a BLT and a ginger ale very slowly. Around twelve, the place starts to fill up. The waitress indicates, through silent glares, that I am jeopardizing her retirement by hogging a table, so I leave. As I'm wandering the streets of Manhattan, I remember the text from Tommy Knutson. Out of curiosity, I retrieve it.

What R U wearing

Oh please.

I head to a Barnes & Noble café and slouch at a table littered with coffee cups and a stack of books on interior design. I'm not hungry, and I don't want to read anything. All I want is to be communicating with Ramie. In person, over the phone, through smoke signals, I don't care.

To pass the time, I scan through all the texts Jill has saved in our cell phone. Most of them are from Ramie arranging different places to meet up. A few are from that Natalie girl. And a handful of cryptic teasers are from Tommy Knutson.

Because I have plenty of time to stew over all of this, I come to the conclusion that in some ways, it's all Tommy Knutson's fault. Oh, shut up, it is. Jill never would have gotten herself drunk and dragged that loser back to the roof if it weren't for Tommy Knutson. She's trying to get over him. That's what all this slutting around with the dregs of Williamsburg is about.

Oh, I'm sorry, did I say slut? I meant *vamp*.

The stupid thing about it is the fact that Jill thinks getting over Tommy Knutson is the best way to get him back. She thinks that after "finding himself" in San Francisco, he'll return to Brooklyn, take one look at her newfound vampy uber-sophistication, and be instantaneously enslaved.

Of course, what *I* think the Great Knutsack is going to find in San Francisco is a city full of boy candy and a diminishing need for girls.

What? You didn't think of that? Man, are you naïve. But don't beat yourself up over it. Jill's only semi-aware of this likelihood herself. In fact, for someone who spends so much time dwelling on Tommy Knutson, she's surprisingly ignorant about him. I should charge her a hundred dollars an hour for my insights.

Anyway, the worst part of all this vamping-around malarkey is the fact that Ramie's completely on board with it. She thinks it's "freeing."

Freeing?

Do these girls not know who is out there? It's all fine and dandy to hang around in the girls' room strategizing slick ways to get boys to kiss you. But out in the real world, there are Larsons and Sashas. There are guys named Permascrew and whole hosts of other things to fear and loathe.

We're not in Winterhead anymore.

My cell phone chirps with another message, but it's not from Ramie. It's from Tommy.

Speaking of things to fear and loathe.

Desert overkill. Much sand.

What is that, poetry?
I text back:

(re)cycler

Dude were thru. Stop messing with head. Im scrwing someone else.

I get up and start roaming around the aisles of Barnes & Noble. For the free heat more than the books. My phone chirps with another message from Tommy.

Hi Jack rough day? Wanna chat?

Oh, excellent. My girlfriend's cheating on me, my alter ego is playing tongue lacrosse with the dregs of Brooklyn, and her gay boyfriend is trying to be my pal. I text back:

No

Thirty seconds later he texts:

Sorry tell Jill I miss her.

That's it. I stalk over to the empty math section, then sit down on the floor and dial Tommy directly.

"Jack?" he says.

"Listen," I say. "You made up your mind when you left Brooklyn, okay? Leave the poor girl alone."

"What's wrong?" he says. "Is she okay?"

"Yes," I say. "She's fine."

"Is she really—"

"Having sex with someone else?" I say. "No. I made that up."

I hear him sigh. "Is she mad at me?"

I lean against the bookshelf. "Ow." The bag presses into my back. "Of course she's mad at you."

"Why?"

I sit cross-legged. "For leaving her in Brooklyn, Einstein."

"What do you mean?" he says. "I invited her to come with me. If anything, she left me."

"Oh, right," I say. " 'Cause it was really an option for us to drive across the country with you. Be real. Anyway, you need to work this out with her 'cause I've got my own problems, okay?"

"What problems?" he says.

"Forget it," I say. "You don't have to pretend to care. Just go back to your desert and whatever it is you're doing."

"Why do you hate me so much?"

"I don't hate you," I say. "I just—" A couple of nerdy teenagers peer into the aisle, then move along. I figure they need the math section more than I do, so I move to the social sciences section.

"Look, Knutson," I say. "We've got kind of a full plate, Jill and me. New York is taking some getting used to. The last thing we need is for you to keep alive a relationship that's obviously doomed. Show some mercy. Let the poor girl go."

"Oh," he says. "I didn't know it was—"

My phone chirps again, and this time it *is* Ramie. Calling, not texting!

"I gotta go," I say. I hang up and take Ramie's call.

"Hi," she says. She sounds mad.

"Where are you?" I stand up and rush to the exit.

"I have class in ten minutes," she says.

Weaving aggressively among slow-moving book browsers, I push my way out the door and head straight for the FIT campus. "Yeah, but where are you right now?" I ask.

The sidewalks are crowded with people who do not appreciate the urgency with which I need to see Ramie face to face.

"Jack," she says. "I can't believe you actually thought I slept with that guy."

"So you didn't?" I stop and nearly collapse from relief. "Thank God. Where are you?"

"I'm right here."

I look up, and there she is, standing on the corner of Twenty-seventh and Seventh. I close my cell phone, run to her, and throw my arms around her.

"Jack," she says. "Wait."

I pull away and look at her.

"How could you think that?" she says.

"Ramie," I say. "All I know is what Jill saw. You were flirting with that guy. You took his hand and led him away."

"Yeah," she says. "I wanted to give Jill some privacy. I brought him downstairs and sent him home."

"Did you kiss him?"

Ramie's face screws up.

"Well, did you?"

"Of course not!"

"Well, how am I supposed to know that?"

"You're supposed to trust me," she says.

"Oh."

"Jack," she says. "Is this how it's going to be? Are you going to wake up every cycle, rummage through Jill's memories, then accuse me of stuff I didn't do?"

"Are you going to spend all your time picking up guys?"

"I didn't pick him up!" she says. "I was being a good wing-man."

"Yes," I say. "Good plan, Rames. Not so convincing, how-ever, as I not only remember you saying 'wingman'; I also re-member you making sure Jill heard it so I'd dig it out of her memory. I'm not stupid."

Ramie stares at me.

"What?" I say.

She keeps staring. Then she leans to the side, just like Al-varez did, to spot Jill's bag protruding from my back.

"It's stuck," I say. "I was in a hurry. Ramie, listen. Do you even know who you were playing *wingman* with?"

"What do you mean?"

I take a deep breath and let it out. "Remember those guys I told you about. The ones I met at Dexter's?"

She looks suddenly worried.

"Ian?" I say. "That's Larson. And the other guy? Sasha? The chubby guy you thought was cute? His name was on that chart too."

Her eyes widen.

"Oh, and remember the blond guy and the black dude?" I say. "You know, the *other* guy you thought was cute that night?"

Ramie only stares at me with this stunned expression.

"The two guys talking to Larson and Sasha," I say. "Remember? When you came out of the girls' room?"

She nods.

"Permascrew," I say. "And Alvarez."

She looks traumatized.

"That's right, Rames. You really picked a pair of winners."

"I can't believe it," she says.

"Me neither," I say. "And incidentally, even Jill thought you were flirting."

"No she didn't."

"Yes she did," I say. "While she was getting felt up by Larson, she still had time to wonder why you were letting Sasha spit so much game at you."

"He wasn't spitting game!"

"Oh, and nice flirtatious fake laugh by the way."

"Stop it."

"You were drunk, Ramie. What if he tried to force himself on you?"

"Stop it!" She drops her head into her hands. "I can't have you spying on me!"

"It's not spying," I say. "It's called memory."

She looks up, her eyes narrowing as she dissects and evaluates me. Then, in a detached monotone, she says, "I have to go to class."

She turns to go, but I grab her gently by the arm. When her eyes laser in on my hand, I release her.

"Sorry," I say. "Can we just—"

"I have to go," she says. "I'll be back around eight."

"You have class until eight?"

"I'm studying with some people," she says. "I have a big test on Monday."

"What people?" I say. "What test? How do you test fashion?"

Ramie just looks at me.

"I'm not spying," I say. "I'm just . . . curious."

"You have no idea what I do," she says. "No idea at all, do you?"

"What do you mean?"

"The test is on eighteenth-century textiles. The people are students in my class. And you test fashion the same way you test any academic subject."

"Sorry," I say.

"Do you want to chaperone us?"

Truthfully? Yes.

But I don't admit to this. Nor do I admit to being as ignorant about her studies as she thinks I am. I mean, I listen when she tells me about her schoolwork. I just don't absorb it all. You'd have to have memory stores even bigger than my own to absorb it all. She talks about it a lot. Is forgetting a few things here and there such a crime?

Maybe it's not a crime. But all of a sudden the fact that I distrusted her does feel like a crime. And the way she's looking at me, as if I were a cop or a spy, makes me wonder if that's what I've become.

"I guess I'll see you tonight," I say. I turn to go.

"Wait," she says.

I stop walking but keep my eyes on the sidewalk.

"Look at me," she says.

But how can I look at her when I know she's right? I *am* a spy. I've been spying on Ramie all my life. Ever since I woke up, I've spent most of my time scouring Jillspace for memories of her. Only now there's so little to recall. Now there are long swaths of time where Jill doesn't even know where Ramie is.

"What's happening to us?" she says.

"I miss you," I say. "The summer was so amazing, and now I hardly see you anymore. I know I shouldn't scrounge through Jillspace for memories of you. I know that makes me a creep and a spy, but mal, Rames, it's all I have."

She smiles. "You said mal."

"What?"

"You never say mal."

"Oh."

"Sometimes . . ." She takes a deep breath. "Sometimes I wish . . ." She stops herself.

"What?" I say. "You wish what?"

She stares at me, an unnameable fear darkening her eyes.

"Tell me," I say.

Ramie looks down. "It doesn't matter," she says. "What I want is impossible anyway."

I step close to her. "Nothing's impossible." I find myself linking pinkies with her. She looks at our hands and smiles. Then she looks up at me.

"I want more," she says.

"More what?"

She bites her lip. "More of *you*," she says.

I put my forehead to hers. "Rames," I say. "You have no idea how much I want that."

"I feel guilty just thinking this," she says. "I love Jill too, you know."

I pull back and look at her. "She knows," I say. "And she won't remember this conversation anyway."

This doesn't comfort her. Nor do I fully believe it. Jill remembers more and more of my life all the time. She may very well remember this conversation.

"I guess some things *are* impossible," I say.

Ramie nods, then brings her lips very gently to mine. Our pinkies are still linked. "When I'm through with school," she says, "I'll never work when you're around."

"Promise?"

She nods.

"And we'll have sex all day?"

She nods again.

I pull her close so that our bodies are touching. Then I bring my lips to her ear. "Come home with me now."

She squirms away. "I can't. I have to go to class."

I groan painfully.

"Don't," she says. "I really need to focus. School's a lot harder than I thought it would be, and there's this teacher's assistant who's recruiting for junior stylist assistants. I think she likes me, so I sort of need to impress her."

"Nerd."

She hits me playfully. "Spy," she says. "Come on. Walk with me."

We head down the sidewalk, pinkies still linked.

"Maybe I'll just study at home tonight," she says.

"Good idea."

"But you can't be molesting me the whole time."

"Can you study naked?"

She laughs. "All right. But you have to go out and get pizza. From the good place."

"With the mean lady?"

"Yes."

Ramie stops in front of a glass-fronted building with a wide bank of marble steps. "Please don't be jealous, Jack. You know you don't have to." She swings our arms out playfully. "You're my one and only."

"I am?"

She nods. "There's no one else like you," she says. "No one in the world."

"So you keep saying."

"Hey." She whacks me on the shoulder. "We fight pretty well."

"Dude," I say. "I was going easy on you."

"Liar." She tugs herself free from my grip and heads up the steps to the building. On the top step, she turns around and smiles at me.

I have loved that smile for as long as I can remember. It is the most radiant object in the universe. Brighter than the moon on a cloudless night. Hotter than the sun at noon. I spent all summer learning its contours and nuances. I could draw it from memory if I knew how to draw.

But there's something unfamiliar about it now, a dimming in the eyes, a knowingness. That's the thing about Ramie. Just when you think you have her figured out, she does something to confound you.

I even love *that* about her.

october 9

●

Jill

"They trade girls?" I ask.

At the kitchen counter, Ramie pulls the peppermint tea bags from two mugs while yawning ferociously. "Yup."

"And keep track on a chart?" I ask.

Ramie nods grimly, then brings the mugs over to the coffee table and sits next to me on the couch.

"Are you sure?" I ask. "Are you deeply sure?"

Ramie nods, then grabs my stocking foot and squeezes it. "Don't worry," she says. "You don't need a man to be happy."

"Easy for you to say."

It's Wednesday. Ramie doesn't have class until one o'clock, and my temp agency's getting back to me about a gig at some law firm. That means, for the morning at least, I am free to wallow in the mystery of how Ian could be such a good kisser and so gross at the same time.

"You know what?" Ramie says. "I wish you could meet him."

"Who, Ian?"

"No, Jack," she says. "I wish you could know him like I do."

"No thanks."

She laughs. "You don't know what you're missing," she says.

And here we begin the monthly ritual I call Oh My God I Can't Believe How Amazing and Wonderful Jack Is.

"Did I ever tell you," she says, "that Jack pushed Ian up against a chain-link fence?"

"No."

"Well, he did."

"Why?" I say.

She turns her whole body toward me, like she's about to tell me a ghost story. "He claims he was filled with mindless rage," she says. "Like an animal or something. But I think it was in defense of the female sex. You know, because of the girl-trading? He's deeply a feminist."

I look at her doubtfully.

"What?" she says. "Boys can be feminists."

"Boys are gross."

"Jill," she says. "You know you don't believe that."

"I should," I say.

Ramie stares dreamily over the lip of her cup. "When I first met him, he was so different from you. I mean polar opposites."

"Who, Ian?" I say.

"No, Jack."

I sigh. "Ramie, can we please not do this today? Can we have one day where we don't do this, and can that be today?"

"Do what?"

"What we always do," I say. "Namely, you rambling on and

on about how amazing and wonderful Jack is while I suppress the gag reflex."

Ramie stares at me in silence for a second, then takes a sip of scalding tea. "Why are you so resistant to him? You have a lot in common, you know. More and more all the time, in fact."

"That's doubtful."

"You see?" she says. "You *are* resistant. He's resistant to you too. You even have *that* in common."

"So we *are* doing this today," I say. "Okay, fine. Let's just spend the rest of our lives talking about Jack Jack Jack!"

"I'm just trying to help," she says. "You know I'm involved in this too."

"Uh, really? Gee, Rames, thanks for reminding me. I think a quarter of a nanosecond passed when I wasn't hyperaware of the all-consuming pervitude of my existence. I think, in fact, the usual everyday pervitude of my existence was temporarily set aside to make room for a new pervitude involving a girl-trader who felt me up last week. But if you want to return to the usual everyday pervitude, fine."

"This is exactly what I'm talking about," she says. "It's like you *need* to believe that Jack is this disgusting interloper in your life. When, in fact, he's—"

"Amazing and wonderful?" I say.

"Mal," she says. "Sometimes you can be so obtuse." She turns her body away and slumps over her mug of tea.

"What does that mean?"

"Look it up," she says. "And while you're at it, look up selfish too."

"Selfish?" I say.

"Yes," she says. "Characterized by a total lack of concern for other people's feelings."

"*I'm* selfish?" I say. "Ramie, I gave up Tommy Knutson for Jack."

Ramie glances at me over the wispy steam from her mug, but she keeps her body turned away.

"I should be driving to San Francisco right now," I say. "But instead, I'm working as a stupid temp secretary so Jack can be with you. So don't try to guilt me out about how unfair it is for poor Jack, who only has four days per—"

All of a sudden the faintest outline of a memory slips across the border between Jack's life and my own.

A discussion of time.

"What's wrong?" Ramie says.

I stare into the calm surface of my peppermint tea.

Ramie and Jack were standing outside that FIT building. It was cold, and Jack was being partially strangled by my green bag.

I turn to Ramie. "I want more."

"More what?" she says. "More tea?"

"More of you," I say.

"Huh?"

"That's what you said to me. I mean to him. You want more of him and less of me."

"I never said that," she says.

"I feel guilty just thinking this," I say.

"Why?" she says.

"No, dumbass. That's what *you* said. You feel guilty because you want less of me and more of Jack."

"That's not what I said!"

I put my cup down and stand up. "You *did* say it, Ramie. I remember it."

"But that's not what I meant."

I back away. "I know what you meant."

"Jill!" She gets up and follows me.

I keep backing away. "I know exactly what you meant!" I turn and run into my room, then slam the door and lock it.

In all the time I've been coping with Jack and Ramie's relationship, it never occurred to me that she'd choose him over me. She's *my* BFF. I thought that meant something. I back away from the door and sit on the edge of my bed. Ramie casts a moving shadow under the door as she paces back and forth in front of it.

"Jill," she says. "Just open the door."

But why should I? She'll only try to argue her way out of it. She'll use her powers of persuasion to convince me that I'm being unreasonable. But I'm not being unreasonable. I know what I remember.

Stewing in my anger, I stare at her shadow beneath the door. But after a while the back-and-forth motion of her shadow becomes more compelling. I find it impossible to look away. It lulls me into an unwilling calm, dulling my anger until my breathing becomes quiet and rhythmic.

"Why won't you listen to me?" she says.

Even her voice is fading now, along with all the details of

hard reality. As I slip uncontrollably into the meditative state, I can no longer hold on to the anger. Before I know it, my eyes are closed.

"Jill?" she says.

But I'm only dimly aware of her. The black dot appears in the center of my forehead, then slowly balloons until it surrounds me completely. With no will to resist, I surrender.

The anger is gone now, and I'm floating in a weightless void, held there by the blackness itself.

It is a moment of perfect peace.

Then an image flickers to life. Manhattan. That sidewalk near FIT. I can feel the cold against Jack's skin. I feel his sadness, his hunger.

Ramie is looking at us with eyes full of longing. "I want more of you," she says.

Their foreheads touch. It's warm and smooth, and I can feel Jack's love for her as a physical entity, something that resides in the body as much as the mind. It's different from the way I loved Tommy Knutson. Simpler, steadier. There is no hesitation or doubt. But something about it hurts.

There's never enough of it.

Suddenly everything goes black. The image and the feelings disappear.

I find myself staring at my bedroom door, Ramie's shadow passing underneath. Back and forth. Back and forth. I try to ride the lulling motion back into the meditative state. I close my eyes and lie down on the bed. I think of the heat where their foreheads touched, the smooth connection of skin on skin. All I want is to feel that love again. There was such honesty to it, such physicality. But all I get is the black dot. For twenty deep breaths I lie there silently repeating the words *I am Jack McTeague,* hoping it will guide me back into his world.

But the black dot yields nothing else. That simple, white-hot love is just a memory. Eventually the rhythmic creaking of Ramie's footsteps outside my room consumes all of my attention.

"You don't understand," she says, her voice muffled behind the door.

But I *do* understand. I understand more clearly than I ever have. Of course Ramie wants more of Jack and less of me. Who wouldn't want to bathe in the heat of that love? Ramie is the whole world to Jack. She's the owner of his soul. What do I give her that compares with that? Half the rent?

I sit up suddenly and face the mirror, my jagged hair poking out all over the place. I look ridiculous. I'm not amazing and wonderful. I'm just a girl with stupid hair. I'm no force of raw animal passion. I've never pushed anyone up against a chain-link fence in defense of the female sex. I've never defended anything. My only contribution to the world is a pile of spreadsheets.

I should lock myself in this room and let Jack take over. It's not as if the world would miss me. Let someone else type spreadsheets.

In fact, let *Jack* type spreadsheets for a while. Yeah. That's right. Let *Jack* pay half the rent.

I turn and face the closed door. "Hey, you know what?" I say.

"What?" Ramie's muffled voice says.

"Maybe Jack can *afford* to be amazing and wonderful because he has no other responsibilities. Did you ever think of that?"

"Jill," she says. "Just open the door."

"I bet he wouldn't be so amazing if he had to work as a temp secretary. I bet he wouldn't be so wonderful if someone broke his heart."

"Ji—i—ill," she whines. "Open the stupid door." I can hear her slide down it and slump onto the floor.

"Do you think he'd still be amazing and wonderful if he found out his new crush was a girl-trader? Because I don't think he would. I think he'd track Ian down and do something not very amazing or wonderful at all."

"Why are you doing this?" she says.

"In fact, when you really stop and think about it," I say. "Jack's had it easy."

"Easy?" she says.

"Yeah," I say. "He's never had to work. He's never had to take the SATs. He didn't even have to go through childhood. And childhood's no picnic, you know."

"I know," she says. "Childhood can be hard."

"Not if you're Jack McTeague, it isn't. If you're Jack McTeague, you get to skip all of that. You just *appear* one day, stalk someone else's BFF for a while, then wake up in an apartment someone else is paying for."

"That's a bit of a simplification," she says, her voice still muffled.

"Still," I say. "How come he gets to have a relationship and I don't? How come he never gets dumped for the sake of a stupid road trip? How come he never makes out with guys who turn out to be girl-traders?"

"Jill," she says. "You're becoming a complainer."

"What!"

I look in the mirror, and lo and behold, two scowl lines have appeared right between my eyebrows! I rub at them with my thumb.

"And you know," Ramie says, "Jack's the one who told me about the chart. You should be *thanking* him."

I freeze with my thumb between my eyebrows as a fresh thought occurs to me. I jump off the bed and jerk the door open, causing Ramie to tumble across the threshold. "Did you actually see this alleged chart?" I ask.

Ramie looks up at me and shakes her head.

"Because I didn't see any chart when I mined Jack's memories."

"What?" She stands up. "How much can you remember?"

"Some!" I say. "And I don't remember a chart. So all we have is Jack's word."

"Why would he lie?"

"I don't know," I say. "To keep you away from Sasha? He knows you were flirting with him."

"I was *not* flirting with Sasha," she says. "I was being a good wingman."

"Right," I say. I walk back into my room and sift through the pile of clothes on my dresser.

"What are you doing?" she says.

I throw on some jeans and the red pouffy blouse, which is wrinkled, but it's the only clean top I can find. I tuck my jagged hair into the wig and secure it with a few hairpins.

"Where are you going?" she says.

I grab my coat and the big green bag, then head to the door.

"Jill!" she shouts.

But I don't answer her.

I'm on a reconnaissance mission.

Ian is not at Dexter's, but his friend, the cute black guy, is. I order a coffee from Joel and sit next to him at the bar.

"Hi," I say. "I'm Jill. Ian's friend?"

He looks at me and nods slowly. "Alvarez." He shakes my hand.

Alvarez. The name sounds dimly familiar.

"By any chance," I say, "are you meeting Ian here?"

"Yup." He takes a sip of his coffee. "You looking for him? There's an epidemic of people looking for Ian Larson these days."

"Can I ask you a question, Alvarez?"

The bartender hands me my coffee and I pour some milk into it.

"Sure," Alvarez says.

I stir the coffee and have a sip. I'm getting used to the bitter taste of New York coffee. It's not so bad with four sugars and a lot of milk. "I was wondering," I say. "Do you and Ian trade girls?"

Alvarez rolls his eyes. "Aw, man."

"Is that a yes?"

Alvarez looks at his wrist. There's no watch there. He takes one last sip of coffee, then slides off the stool. "Sorry," he says. "I gotta run." He puts a five-dollar bill on the bar and rushes out the door while sliding into his coat.

Joel the bartender comes over. "Are those guys being dicks?"

"Possibly," I say.

I don't want to describe the chart to him, because I'm hoping it's an ugly story Jack made up to keep Ramie away from Sasha.

"*Someone* is being a dick," I say. "I'm not entirely sure who."

Joel nods slowly. "Well," he says, "I hate to say this, but if I were you, I wouldn't give *those* guys the benefit of the doubt."

"Why?"

"I don't know that Larson guy very well. And Alvarez seems okay. But their friend, that little blond guy? Pure scum."

"Really?"

He rests an elbow on the bar. "He dated this friend of mine, and when she dumped him, he went completely apeshit on her. Started following her around and calling her at work. Scary dude. I asked my boss if I could eighty-six him, but he spends a lot of money here. Trust fund kid."

"A trustafarian?" I say.

"Yeah." He laughs. "He's always buying rounds. That's probably why they hang out with him."

Interesting. It certainly indicts the blond guy, but all it says about Ian is that he has bad taste in friends. That's not a hanging offense.

"Oh," Joel says. "And the four of them keep a chart of all the girls they've slept with."

I almost choke on the coffee. "You know about that?"

"They sit right there." He points to a table by the window. "They don't exactly hide it. I think it's that little blond guy's thing. What's his name? Permafrost or something?"

The memory drifts up suddenly from Jacktime. "Perma-screw," I say. There's a story behind the name, and I have to focus to uncover it. "Because . . ." I close my eyes and concentrate, the hazy image of the blond guy sharpening. "Because when he screws a girl, she stays screwed."

"He said that?" Joel asks.

"Yes!" I nod excitedly because I just excavated a complete Jackmemory with the sheer force of my own mind. Wow!

And yuck.

"Well, it's probably none of my business," Joel says, "but I think you can do better than that."

"Really?"

He nods, then wipes down the bar and stacks up some discarded newspapers. "You've got that fresh-scrubbed small-town thing going for you."

"But I was going for vamp."

Joel laughs, then, realizing I was serious, looks embarrassed. "Oh, I mean, um . . ."

"It's okay," I tell him. "I'm still working on it."

"Of course." His face darkens suddenly as he sees something at the door.

Turning around, I spot Ian entering. When he sees me, he

takes a small step backward, as if hoping to make a speedy exit.

"Wait," I say to him. I turn to Joel. "How much for the coffee?"

Joel shakes his head. "On me."

"You don't have to do that."

"It's provisional," he says.

"On what?"

"On you doing better for yourself."

What a sweet thing to say. Or is Joel flirting with me?

"Deal," I say.

I grab my coat and bag and head to the door. Ian stands there awkwardly, half blocking my exit. I push the door open and go outside. Ian hesitates in the doorway for a second, then follows me outside.

"One question," I say.

He stands in front of me, slouching nervously, his breath fogging in the cold.

"Is my name on that chart?"

"What?" he says. "No! Of course not. Listen, tell your brother . . ."

"My brother?" I say.

"Isn't he your brother?" he says. "He said he was your brother."

"Oh," I say. "Yeah. Never mind my brother, Ian. Is it true? Do you and your friends . . ." I have to take a deep breath before I say it aloud. "Do you trade girls?"

"It's not like that," he says.

"Really?" I say. "What is it like?"

Ian stares at me for a few seconds, then sighs and looks at the ground.

"So it *is* like that," I say.

He shrugs.

"Do you even know how gross that is?"

When he looks up at me, he *seems* sorry, even if he doesn't come out and say it. Sorry and cute, actually. But that's an absurd thing to be thinking right now. I should be shoving him against that wall or, at the very least, scorching him with a blistering retort. Unfortunately, all I can think of is how naughty and delicious it felt when he put his hand up my shirt. Mal, I'm such a pervert.

I steel myself.

"Yeah, well . . . ," I say. "I . . . I . . . I was just using you anyway."

"You were?" he says. "For what?"

I want to tell Ian I was using him for sex, because I'm pretty sure that's what a vamp would say, but I can't seem to get the words out. My face grows hot, and I know it's turning red. It's so frustrating. What's the point of becoming an uber-sophisticated New York City vamp if you can't turn it into a weapon?

"Hey, maybe we should—" he says.

"Shut up!" I say. Then I turn and run away.

"Wait!" he says.

But I don't wait, and he doesn't follow. By the time I get to McCarren Park, I'm running and crying like a stupid baby! I run home as fast as I can with the goal of locking myself in my bedroom forever. But when I get through the door, despite the fact that I'm still mad at her, I find myself calling out Ramie's name. She may be a disloyal friend who's choosing Jack over me, but she's all I have in this ugly girl-trading world.

She comes out of her bedroom half dressed, shoving an earring into one ear. "Are you okay?" she says.

I wipe my runny nose. "I hate this city. I hate this world."

Ramie rushes to me.

"Stop," I say.

She freezes.

"Technically, I'm still mad at you," I say.

"Why?"

"For trying to kill me."

"Jill." She walks right up to me. "My love, if I were trying to kill you, you'd already be dead."

"Don't make jokes." I sniffle.

"But you can't be serious," she says. "You know I'd be lost without you."

"Really?"

She hooks her pinkie with mine. "Of course."

I suppose I *do* know, on some level, but I'm still mad at her. Maybe that's because deep down I can't help but agree that when all is said and done, Jack *is* more amazing and wonderful than I am. Maybe he deserves to have a relationship; whereas I deserve to be dropped off in Brooklyn and felt up by girl-traders.

"Did you see Ian?" she asks.

I nod.

"And?"

"Why did he have to be such a good kisser?" I say.

Ramie hugs me. "You don't need him," she says. She pulls back and brushes the wig hair from my eyes. "He's nothing. He's a tiny speck of dirt. You can do so much better than him."

"That's what Joel said."

"The cute bartender?" she says.

I sniffle. "You think he's cute?"

Ramie smiles and leans back to evaluate me. "Now, that's what I'm talking about. Line them up and check them off. Ian is so last month. And we do not get hung up on boys from our past, do we?"

I shake my head.

"Correct answer," she says. "Come here. I want to show you something." She drags me into her bedroom.

"Ramie, please don't dress me up like a clown today. I deeply can't handle it right now."

"Shh," she says. "Look."

She makes me stand in front of her full-length mirror next to the one-armed mannequin. I have no makeup on, and my wig is a tangled mess.

"I went out like this," I say.

"Shut up," she says. "You look gorgeous." She stands behind me and cinches the red satin blouse in the back to make it tighter. "You've lost some weight," she says.

"No thanks to you and Jack," I say. "Do you think the guy could manage to consume a single vegetable? All he ever eats is pizza."

"And kielbasa," she says. "I guess he does rely on you to provide his essential nutrients."

"And his cash and a roof over his head."

"You're right. He's pretty ungrateful. I'll have a word with him about it."

"I bet that'll go over well."

She puts her finger to my lips. "Shh," she says. "We're not talking about Jack today. We're talking about you." She reaches up for my wig.

I grab her hand. "What are you doing?"

She pushes my hand away gently. "Trust me." She takes the wig off and places it carefully on the one-armed mannequin. Then she runs her fingers through my hair to mess it up. "You see? You look *well fit* with short hair."

"Well fit?" I say. "What does that mean?"

"It means hot," she says. "It's British slang. I learned it from Marguerite, my TA in textile history. She's English. Hold on." She rummages through her overflowing closet and comes out with a thick red patent leather belt. She wraps it around my waist. "See that?" she says. "Instant sex bomb." She lifts my head up and makes me look at myself in the mirror again.

I've never worn such a tight belt before. "You really like it?" I ask.

"Defo," she says. "Don't lose any more weight, though."

"Defo?" I say. "Is that British slang too?"

Ramie nods. "According to Marguerite, the whole fashion industry is run by the British mafia. She should know. She's practically part of it now."

"The fashion industry has a mafia?"

"Yeah, not a literal mafia." She pulls a long string of pink and black beads from her drawer. "They don't kill people for bad runway shows or anything." She drapes it around my neck.

"How cool would that be, though?"

Ramie laughs. "Yeah." She holds an imaginary machine gun and points it at her closet. "Pleats! Prepare to die!"

"No way," I say. "The mafia would be way more secretive. They'd make people die of starvation or overdose. Something that couldn't be traced back to them."

"Devious," she says.

"Yeah." I keep my eyes on the mirror. "But I've got that small-town thing working for me, right?"

Ramie drops onto the edge of the bed to evaluate me. "I'm not getting small town so much. Not anymore."

"Good," I say. "That was defo last month." I double the string of beads around my neck. Then I put my hands on my hips and strike a pose. "Do I look like a vamp?"

She shakes her head.

"Well, what do I look like?"

She cocks her head to the side. "You look like you."

"Only better?" I ask.

She smiles mysteriously, but she doesn't answer.

I decide (after the fact, admittedly) that ditching the wig is a symbolic act. A sloughing off of the old me to reveal the shinier me underneath. I am committed now to becoming at least as Amazing and Wonderful as Jack, but in my own inimitable way, whatever that is. A wigless head is defo the first step. Plus, that thing itched like a nest of fleas.

Ian is behind me, a mere blip in my ongoing journey to become Amazing and Wonderful. It was foolish to think I needed a boy to distract me from another boy. It all adds up to an excess of boy in your life. For now, I am taking a vacation from boy obsession in order to cultivate the dignity of singlehood. Who knows where it will lead.

So one morning I'm making my way from the subway to some law firm downtown when my mom calls.

"We were thinking of visiting," she says.

What I hear is: free dinner and a mother-daughter bonding session through Mastercard and Filene's Basement.

"Wait," I say. "Did you say *we*?"

"Would that be okay?" she says. "Don't worry, we'll stay in a hotel. But we'd like to see your apartment."

"Sure," I say. "Are you and Dad, like, getting along now?"

"Things are changing," she says. "But don't get your hopes up. He's still Dad."

Helen McTeague, ladies and gentlemen, fountain of optimism.

When I get off the phone, I realize this is a perfect opportunity to show off the new me. It'll be like an audition, but a safe one. After all, they're my parents. They *have* to love me.

That night, while Ramie sits on the living-room floor tearing out pages of a magazine and putting them into piles representing "crap," "shit," and "genius," for some extracurricular project she's doing with that TA, Marguerite, I take a good, hard look at our apartment. Our coats sit in a pile by the door. There are old copies of *The Village Voice* everywhere, plus empty soda cans, pizza boxes, small piles of loose change, and a minefield of dried tea bags scattered about. A pale gray layer of dust blankets all horizontal surfaces, and the kitchen floor is splattered with a variety of spilled liquids.

"Jeeze, Rames," I say. "We live like bears."

She looks up from her magazine, glances around, then shrugs.

"We need to not live like bears, because my parents are visiting."

"Both of them?"

I nod. "Apparently, things are changing. But seriously, Rames, if my mom sees this, she'll chloroform me, then stuff me into a windowless van and drag me back to Winterhead."

"I deeply believe that," she says. "Okay. Can we afford a cleaning lady?"

"Doubtful," I say. "Besides, aren't we a little young to have servants?"

She neatens up her piles of magazine pages. "They're not servants, Jill. They're, like, independent contractors. Hey, I know. I bet if we put our pictures up on craigslist, we could get some guy to come over and clean our apartment for free."

"Aces, Rames. Then he can violently stab us to death."

"Pessimist."

•

The next day, we head to the supermarket for some cleaning products and a six-pack of beer, which the Polish checkout girls sell me without even hesitating. It must be my new wigless look. I swear I can pass for twenty-one now, maybe even twenty-two. I don't even like beer, but I get a thrill out of buying it.

As we're walking home from the supermarket, my cell phone chirps with another text from the ever-mysterious Tommy Knutson:

Grand canyon. Not so grand.

I show Ramie. She shrugs. I shrug too, but it's forced and she knows it. Though I am committed to a boy-free interval to allow the shinier new me to shine, I still get excited by Tommy's texts. I've stopped looking for coded "I love you's" in them, because that's pathetic, but I have not been able to resist keeping a mental tally of their growing infrequency. Twice a day has slipped to once or twice *a week*. I don't know if this means that he's getting over me or that he wants me to *think* he's getting over me. Boys can be treacherous.

"Are you going to respond?" she asks.

"In forty-eight hours," I tell her.

Ramie shakes her head in disapproval.

"Ramie," I say. "I don't want Tommy to think I'm hanging on every text."

"But you are," she says.

"No way," I say. "I don't need boys. I'm too busy, what with all the gallery openings and movie premieres and leisurely afternoons in various cafés with interesting Europeans and stuff. I simply do not have time to respond to these half-baked texts in a timely manner."

"You are a complete fraud," she says.

"Plus," I say, "forty-eight hours gives me time to come up with something achingly casual."

"Jill," she says. "When I said you should get over the boys from your past, I didn't mean you should *pretend* to get over them. I meant you should actually get over them."

"Haven't you ever heard of fake it till you make it?"

Ramie rolls her eyes. But she doesn't understand, because her love life is simple. Whatever she and Jack feel about each other, they just come out and *say*. That's fine for them, but out here in the real world, where I live, things are *complex*.

When we get back home, we dive right into the disaster we've created. Honestly, I can't believe we let it get this bad. Who raised us? After an hour of cleaning, we're so covered in muck, we decide to strip down to our underwear. The floor is immune to all mopping, so we resort to scrubbing the mysterious stains with our toothbrushes. It turns into an all-day affair, but just as the sky is turning that lovely violet through the living-room window, we both collapse on the couch to admire our work. The place is spotless. It even smells lemony fresh.

"How long will it stay like this?" I ask.

"Unknown," she says. "I think you have to maintain it.

Maybe we should each have assigned chores. I know. We can make a chart."

"Don't say chart," I tell her.

"Sorry."

On the Saturday Mom and Dad are to arrive, Ramie gets stuck in Manhattan to meet with that Marguerite girl about some "unbelievably wicked" opportunity, which she doesn't want to jinx by describing. This is probably for the best, as there remains a deep reservoir of mal feelings between Ramie and my mom. I understand this now as essentially a competition over influence on my life. I understand a lot of things now, possibly because the loss of the wig is allowing my brain to breathe better.

I get to work doing some "maintenance" on the apartment to make sure it's perfectly spick-and-span. Believe me, nothing would make Mom happier than to find me starving, infested, and sleeping in a cardboard box. But I intend to show both of my parents that I can take care of myself.

When they finally buzz, I'm so nervous my stomach is flipping over. I can't believe I'm this eager to see my *parents*. I check my hair one last time in the mirror, straighten my red corset belt, and prepare to wow them with the new Amazing and Wonderful me.

When I open the door, my mom's smiling this big, beautiful smile, which collapses the second she sees me.

"Oh, dear God," she says.

"What?"

She puts her hand to her heart. "For a second I thought you were Jack."

"What!" I run from the front door, letting it slam right in her face. "Sorry!" I say. I run to the bathroom and turn on the light.

Mom opens the door and creeps in, with Dad behind her. I hear them whispering as I stare at myself in the bathroom mirror.

"Do I really look like Jack?" I call out.

"What did you expect, sweetie?"

I don't know what I expected, but none of my memories of Jack involve him looking in the mirror. I have no idea what he looks like. I run into Ramie's room and dig through her underwear drawer, where she keeps her digital camera. On it are some horrifying photos of the two them doing stuff you really don't want to know about. Eventually I find a close-up of Jack's face and compare it with my own in the mirror.

"Oh mal," I say.

"He's a good-looking kid!" Dad calls out from the living room.

Mom shushes him.

Whether or not Jack is a "good-looking kid" is beside the point. The important thing is that he looks just like me, especially now that we have the same hair. How could I have been so stupid?

I brush my micro bangs from one side to the other, but it's no use. There's not enough hair to work with.

"Honey!" Mom calls out from the living room. "Why don't

you just put the wig back on? It's a quality wig. It cost us a fortune."

"It's too late," I say. "I've already been spotted without it."

I can hear Mom sigh. "Was this Ramie's idea? I can smell Ramie all over this."

She's right, of course. This was *all* Ramie's idea. I could kill her right now, but I don't want to give Mom the satisfaction of being right. I put Ramie's camera back in her underwear drawer and return to the living room.

"Hey, kiddo," Dad says. "I think you look terrific."

As soon as I see him, I freeze. The man standing before me is not my father. He can't be.

"Dad?"

He laughs. "That's my name."

"But—"

His hair is short. His face is shaved. And he's wearing normal khakis, a normal blue sweater, and a normal gray fleece.

"What happened to you?" I say.

"It's a long story," he says. "Do I get a hug? Are we still doing hugs? You're not too old for that, are you?"

I walk over and give him a hug. He smells clean, like shaving cream, which I'm pretty sure is the official smell of normal fathers.

I look to my mom in hope of an explanation, but she is single-mindedly focused on my head, which seems to offend her on a profound level.

"Mom, forget it, okay? The wig's a goner. You're going to have to cope somehow."

Mom nods, but it's more to convince herself than me. "Fine," she says. "It'll be fine. Don't worry. It'll be fine."

"So fine, then?" I say. "We're going with fine? Good." I look at my father. "I don't even know what to say, Dad. You look like . . . like the old Dad."

He smiles.

"Way to upstage me," I tell him. "I was hoping to wow you with the new me."

"We *are* wowed," he says. "You look beautiful, honey." He grabs my chin and wiggles it back and forth. "Doesn't she look beautiful, Helen?"

"You're going to need more makeup," Mom says. "Some blush. Maybe some eyeliner. Come here." She opens her arms, and I give her a hug.

"What's that?" I say. "You think I should buy these incredibly sexy and deeply feminine boots I saw at Filene's Basement? And you want to pay for them yourself?"

Mom pulls away and looks at me. "Fine." She looks around the living room. "So this is it?"

"It's cute," Dad says. "Very tidy."

Mom nods suspiciously. "Did you hire a maid?"

"What! No. Ramie and I are very tidy. Our apartment is *always* this clean."

She nods, but she doesn't believe a word of it.

When I take my parents for a mini-tour of Williamsburg, they seem cautiously enchanted by the place. Dad can't seem to get over how many of the "younger generation" are wearing beards, a disturbing fact I hadn't noticed until now. Mom seems impressed with the general "energy" but skeptical of the actual inhabitants, whom she deems "unkempt."

What's strange to me is the way Mom and Dad look like a married couple again. At one point, while we're waiting for a table at this Japanese restaurant in Manhattan that Natalie recommended, Dad's hand touches hers and she doesn't swat it away.

My parents don't eat sushi, so I have to guide them through the menu. After a few brave but tentative bites, they both decide that raw fish is probably "an acquired taste."

Honestly, my parents can be so provincial. And now that I have the rest of New York City to compare them with, I can't help but notice how unstylish they are. My mom looks like she stepped straight out of a JCPenney catalog, and my dad's wearing *fleece*. I don't think anyone outside of New England wears fleece unless they're climbing a mountain or something. I don't hate my parents for this, though. It's what happens when you live in suburbia for too long, a fate I am already avoiding.

When we've finished eating and the waitress has taken our plates, my mom puts her chopsticks down with mathematical precision. "So," she says. "Let's talk about the plan."

"Well." I put my chopsticks down too. "I was thinking brunch around ten tomorrow and then shopping, and then there's this—"

"Honey," she says. "I'm not talking about tomorrow." She looks at my dad, who presses his lips together seriously. "I'm talking about your future," she says.

"Oh."

"Oh?" Mom says. She faces my father. "Does that sound like a plan to you, Richard?"

Dad laughs and looks at me. "We just want you to be happy."

"I'm happy."

"Are you?" Mom says.

The waitress comes by to refill our water glasses, and we all sit in uncomfortable silence until she leaves.

"You don't think I'm happy?" I ask.

"I don't think you will be for long," Mom says. "Jill, your future doesn't just happen. You have to *make* it happen. Now listen, I've already spoken to the dean at Groton College. He's willing to enroll you next semester. You don't even have to reapply."

"You're not serious," I say.

"I had to fake *another* doctor's note," she says. "Sweetheart, at the rate I'm going, I'll be in jail for forgery soon."

"I'm not going to Groton."

Dad cocks his head at me sympathetically. "You don't like Groton?"

"It's in *Winterhead*," I say.

"Honey," Mom says. "You can't avoid Winterhead forever."

"Why not?"

"Don't be silly," she says. "People have moved on. It's time you did too. It's time to kick-start your future." She accentuates the word "kick" with a gentle punch in the air.

"Yeah, well, I'm not going to Groton, so forget it. And anyway, I promised Ramie I'd live with her for at least a year."

Dad puts his hand on mine. "We just want you to be happy, sweetheart."

"I *am* happy," I say.

The middle-aged couple eavesdropping at the next table look over.

I lower my voice. "I'll go to college. I promise."

"When?" Mom says.

"I don't know yet."

"What's to know?" she says. "Just pick a semester. Spring or fall."

"Okay. Fall."

"Great," Mom says. "That takes care of when. How about where?"

My shoulders slump. I realize that this is going to be the only topic of conversation between my mom and me until I come up with a satisfactory answer. But I don't have a satisfactory answer.

"Um," I say. "NYU?"

"NYU?" she says. "Do you have any idea how expensive NYU is?"

"Columbia?" I say.

Mom sighs in exasperation, then looks at my dad. He pats her hand to calm her down.

"What about a safety school?" she says. "You know, in case you don't win the lottery?"

"Yeah," I say. "I have a safety school."

"Which one?" Mom says.

I try to think of the lamest college I've heard of, but the only thing that comes to mind is the Barbizon School of Modeling, which Ramie and I laugh at every time we see it in the back of a magazine. "Oh, right," I say. "Um, Esswich Agricultural Community College."

"Esswich Aggie?" Mom says. "You're picking Esswich Aggie as your safety school?"

"Mom," I say. "Don't be a snob. Just because it's in Esswich doesn't mean it's a bad school."

Mom's head makes these tiny shaky motions. She always does this when her frustration exceeds the boundaries of decorum. I'm not sure if she's upset by the idea of my obtaining an associate's degree in animal husbandry or by the fact that I've obviously given no serious thought to my academic future.

But I don't like thinking about my academic future. There are too many unknowns. Anyway, I've had a rough few months, what with my public undoing at the prom and my escape from Winterhead. I've got my hands full earning a living, taking care of Jack, and becoming Amazing and Wonderful. Shouldn't we be focused on *that*?

"I just don't want to see you slipping behind," she says.

"Behind what?" I say.

Mom sighs. It's strange, but she seems to think I'm still in high school and that all of my friends have been promoted whereas I've been left back. But that's not the way it is. I'm living on my own in New York City. That's a kind of promotion, isn't it? I mean, every time I go to the ATM and see my steadily increasing bank balance, I get a thrill. How many college students can say that?

When the check comes, my mom grabs it. "We'll talk about this tomorrow," she says.

"Fine," I say. But I know it won't get us anywhere, because I don't have a college plan and I don't want to make one right now. Maybe I should, but I don't.

Mom's face crinkles up as she looks at the bill. "That's strange," she says. "Over a hundred dollars, and I'm still hungry."

Welcome to New York, I think.

Mom's employer, Parson's Placement Agency, finagled some massive corporate discount at this fancy midtown hotel in the theater district. While Mom checks them in at the reception desk, Dad and I wait beneath an enormous chandelier in the lobby. The place is abuzz with people returning from the theater, clutching programs.

"Maybe we should have gotten tickets to something," I say.

"It's enough just seeing you, kiddo," he says. "Is there anything you need? Anything at all?"

"Nope," I say. "I've got it all under control."

Dad keeps smiling at me with glazed eyes.

"Are you on Prozac?" I ask.

He shakes his head. "Just happy to see you," he says.

"Oh," I say.

He keeps looking at me, and I realize his eyes aren't glazed; they're full of love. Pure, uncomplicated love. The old Dad used to look at me that way when I'd serve him tea with my Barbie tea set. Like I was this rare, precious flower and he couldn't believe how lucky he was to behold it. I never realized how much I missed that Dad.

"Dad?" I ask. "Are you still living in the basement?"

He shakes his head. He opens his mouth as if he's about to say something; then he changes his mind and scruffs up my hair instead.

"What?" I say. "What were you going to say?"

He laughs. Then he takes a deep breath. "I was going to say I'm sorry."

"For what?"

"For the way I bailed out on you and your mother," he says.

"And Jack?" I say.

He nods. "And Jack. Of course."

"Why did you do it?" I say.

He takes another deep breath and looks at the marble floor.

"Go ahead, I can take it," I say.

He nods and wiggles my chin back and forth. "I know you can, honey." He takes a breath. "It wasn't one big mistake. It was a lot of small ones. Little truths I avoided because it was easier just to go along. Take the higher-paying job. Take the promotion. Switch to a field I didn't care much about. It's so easy to do. But then all those mistakes add up, and you find yourself on a precipice, staring into a future you don't even want."

"Are you talking about when you were—"

"On the eve of partnership," he says. "Yes."

How many times did I hear my parents whisper that phrase in anger?

"I hated what I'd become," he says. "And I wasn't even sure how I'd gotten there. It took a lot of time to figure it all out. I know it doesn't justify things, honey. And believe me, I know how hard your mother worked to put me through law school. But—" His eyes flick to my mother, who's making her way toward us with the room key.

"Dad?" I say before she gets to us. "Was marrying Mom one of those mistakes?"

"Oh, princess." He pulls me close and gives me a big hug. "Don't ever think that."

I close my eyes and rest my head on his shoulder, surprised at how relieved I am to hear this. I always suspected my parents would end up divorced. Despite the messed-up, frigid nature of their relationship, I think it would have killed me.

When I pull away from Dad, Mom is staring at us in confusion. "What?" she says. "What's going on?"

Dad looks at me and winks. "Nothing," he says. "Just a good-night hug."

She knows he's lying, but she doesn't push it.

"Good night, honey." She gives me a hug. "We'll come and get you at ten." She heads to the elevator with Dad.

When they step inside, they both turn and wave at me. Dad grabs her hand, and she lets him hold it.

As the doors close on this strange tableau, I can't decide if my parents are becoming less insane or if, instead, their individual insanities have co-evolved to a state of harmonious symbiosis—like a caterpillar and the milkweed on which it grows.

Either way, I like them a lot better like this.

•

As I'm walking home that night, my dad's words keep running through my head. I wonder about all the potential mistakes I've made, like getting rid of my wig and not having sex with Tommy Knutson. Will these add up one day too? Will there be others? I deeply don't want to find myself standing on a precipice staring into a future I don't even want.

Whose basement would I move into?

october 21

●

Jack

The buzzer wakes me from a deep sleep. I don't know what day it is, what time it is, or, at first anyway, where the heck I am. I stumble half blind to the intercom and press the talk button.

"Hello?" I croak.

"Hi, honey!" some woman says. "Can you let us in?"

I step back from the buzzer and stare at it in horror. After a few seconds it buzzes again.

I press the listen button.

"Jill?" she says. "Are you up, honey? Can you let us in?"

In the background, a familiar man's voice says something unintelligible.

I press the talk button. "Um . . ."

"Honey?" she says. "What's wrong?" The woman's voice lowers as she turns away from the intercom. "She sounds ill." Then it gets clear again. "Honey, are you ill?"

I am now.

It takes a moment to summon the relevant Jillmemories to

explain *my parents'* presence in Brooklyn. Critical highlights: they invited themselves for a visit, argued with Jill about her future, then offered to buy her some boots. I was not consulted.

I call out Ramie's name, but there's no answer. When I check her bedroom, it's empty.

What am I supposed to say to my parents? I hate them. They locked me in a room, remember? But they keep buzzing, and I have a feeling if I don't let them in, they'll assume Jill's been taken hostage and call the police. Simultaneously resigned to and regretting the decision, I buzz them in.

While I'm staring at the door, Jillmemories begin to swirl around in my head. She had plans for today and for several days thereafter. I've come early again. I've come very early.

It's only when I hear their footsteps approaching that I look down and realize I'm wearing Jill's pink Tinker Bell pajamas. They knock on the door and I open it.

Mom and Dad look at me, then look at each other, then look at me again.

"Jack?" Dad says.

"Yeah?" I say.

"You're wearing makeup," he says. "That's . . . new."

"Oh crap." I grab the bottom of Jill's shirt and start wiping it off, but it stings my eyes. "Hold on," I say. I back away from the door and let Mom catch it. I run to the bathroom to wash the makeup off, then change into some jeans and a T-shirt.

When I return to the living room, it's clear my parents have been whispering heatedly.

"There he is," Dad says, smiling dumbly. His hair is trimmed, his clothes clean, his beard shaved.

"What happened to you?" I ask.

"That's exactly what Jill said."

I hazard a glance at Mom, who looks back in irritated confusion, as if she'd ordered the steak and wound up with sea urchin. "I don't understand," she says. "Jill should have five more days. At *least*."

"Well, don't look at me," I say. "All I did was wake up."

She narrows her eyes. "Well, this is . . ." Her head makes those tiny shaky motions.

Dad watches her nervously for a second, then comes over and punches me on the shoulder. "Heck, I think it's terrific. Do I get a hug? Or is that too much?"

"It's too much," I say.

"Fair enough," he says. "Hey, I know." He claps excitedly. "Why don't we make a day of it!"

Mom looks at him in horror, but he just keeps smiling.

"How about it, Jack?" he says. "Are you hungry? Have you eaten? Why don't we go out for breakfast."

"You want to go out for breakfast?" I say. "With *me*?"

"Why not?" he says. "You've got to eat. What do you say, Helen?"

But Helen seems to have crashed like a piece of buggy software, her body rigid and her face stuck in a permanent expression of disgust and dismay. After a few seconds she reboots and says, "Yes. That would be nice."

"Hah!" I say. Because seriously, nothing would be less "nice" than me and the Evil Snow Queen of Winterhead eating breakfast together. And that's not just *my* opinion. Believe me, this hatred is a two-way affair. What must be happening is that Mom's software is struggling to collate the unexpected data of my presence and has fallen back on an older version that prioritized decorum.

"Actually, you know what?" I say, just to mess with her. "You're right, *Mom*. That *would* be nice."

"Perfect," Dad says. "Where should we go?"

Unlike Dad, Mom understands sarcasm. "Richard," she says. "Maybe we should just go home."

"Wow, that's amazing," I say. "You must be psychic, because I was thinking the exact same thing."

"Now just wait a minute," Dad says. "Let's not be hasty here." He positions himself between Mom and me like a referee in a boxing match. "All I'm suggesting is that we go have a meal together."

"Oh, I get it," I say. "You buy me breakfast and we just pretend the last four years didn't happen?"

Dad shakes his head in big, dramatic arcs. "That's not what I'm suggesting here."

"Look," I say. "Just because I was big enough to be civilized toward you this summer doesn't mean all's forgiven. You guys locked me in a room. Do you remember that?"

"Of course we remember," he says.

"Not like I do," I say. "I remember the smell of paint. And the cameras. I remember the drip from the shower, which, incidentally, was the only sound I heard because of the *metal plates* over the windows and the *locked steel door*."

"We made mistakes," Dad says.

"Don't kid yourself, Dad. Mom made mistakes. All you did was nothing."

"Now wait a minute, Jack. I was the one who showed Jill the code to that security system."

"Yeah, and what was that about anyway?" I say. "What kind of messed-up, indirect—"

"Richard," Mom says. "Let's just go."

"No," Dad says. "We have a lot to talk about. This is good. I think we need this. All feelings are valid here. Let's see if we can't work through it."

"No," I tell him. "You didn't come here to see me. You scheduled this visit for Jill's phase, so let's stop pretending you even care about me. Let's just go back to ignoring each other."

Just then footsteps come rushing up the stairs, followed by keys jingling in the lock. For a crazy second I have visions of Jill coming home and whisking my parents away.

But of course, it's Ramie.

When she comes in the door, she looks as shocked to see me as my parents were.

"Jack!" she says. "What are you doing here?"

"I guess that's the question of the day," I say.

Ramie looks at my parents, then back at me.

"Hi, Ramie," Dad says. "How are you?"

"Great," she says. "Hi, Mrs. McTeague."

"Hello, Ramie," Mom says. Subtext: you are the devil's spawn.

Ramie turns to me. "Big hurry. Can't stay. Come with me?"

I nod, and she drags me into the safe, parent-free sanctum of her room. I close the door and put my back to it.

"I deeply did not expect to see you today," she says.

"Hold me."

She laughs, then gives me a big hug. "There, there." She pulls back. "What happened to your dad? He looks *amazing*."

"Make them leave."

She goes to her closet and drags her suitcase out.

"Where are you going?"

"Marguerite's waiting in a car downstairs," she says. "I'm going to Paris!" She throws the suitcase on the bed and opens it.

"What?" I say. "For how long?"

She looks up and squints painfully. "Five days?"

"But you'll miss my whole phase."

"I know." She opens her dresser drawer and hurriedly pulls underwear and socks out of it. "I'll be back Thursday night. I didn't think you'd be here yet."

"But I *am* here," I say.

She throws the underwear and socks into the open suitcase. "Jack," she says. "We're shooting Paris *Vogue*. I'm assisting Marguerite, who's assisting Marley Storm-Anders." She opens another drawer and takes out some T-shirts.

"Who's Marley Storm-Anders?"

Ramie pauses for a moment to express her shock at my ignorance of this apparent celebrity, then rushes to her closet and starts rifling through it at warp speed. "Only the third-biggest stylist in the industry. I know I've mentioned her before." She pulls out a pair of black jeans.

"Oh," I say. I do not bother pretending to be impressed by this, because all of my energy is consumed by my furious opposition to her being anywhere but at my side right now.

She rolls up the jeans, then presses them into the suitcase. "It's big," she says. "Trust me. These are the kinds of connections you can only get through people like Marguerite. She knows *everybody*. I mean, people really doing it, you know?"

"Doing what?"

"*It,*" she says. She zips up her bag and kisses me on the lips.

"Marguerite," I say. "Is she that teacher's assistant? That English girl you told Jill about?"

Ramie nods. "She's brilliant. You'll love her." She drags her suitcase off the bed. "Come on, I have to hurry."

She wheels her suitcase through the door and out to the living room, with me following close on her heels.

At the front door, she faces my parents. "Sorry I missed you yesterday. You look great, Mr. McTeague. I like your haircut."

So help me God, my father blushes. "Thanks," he says. "It's good to see you, Ramie."

Mom smiles her preprogrammed tolerance-only smile.

The sight of both of them side by side on my couch makes me shudder. When Ramie opens the door to leave, I follow her down the stairs.

Outside, a black airport limo awaits. In the backseat is a beautiful redhead talking on a cell phone while madly scribbling in a notebook. Marguerite, presumably. Her bright blue scarf blows through the half-opened window. She doesn't look at us.

The driver puts Ramie's suitcase in the trunk, and Ramie comes over for a final kiss.

"Don't go," I say.

"You don't mean that," she says. "Because you know how important this is to me."

"No I don't."

Marguerite knocks on the window, then motions for Ramie to join her quickly. She never looks at me.

"I have to go," Ramie says. "Wish me luck." She kisses me on the forehead, then gets into the car. Marguerite, still absorbed by her phone call, moves an expensive-looking bag off the seat and makes room for Ramie. Ramie rolls down the window all the way. "Hey, maybe you should just make up with your parents," she says.

"Why?"

She shrugs. "Something different."

"Never," I say.

She shakes her head.

"I love you," I say.

Ramie opens her mouth, but the car drives off before she can say anything. There's a blinding glare on the rear window, so I can't tell if she's waving or mouthing "I love you too." I watch her car disappear around a corner; then I stare at the corner that swallowed it.

I wonder what made Ramie think I'd "love" Marguerite. Sure she's beautiful. I guess that counts for something. But she didn't even have the decency to introduce herself to me. Was her phone call *so* important? Was there a global fashion crisis she had to fix? I wonder if Marguerite even knows who I am. I wonder if Ramie's told her anything about me, like, for example, that I'm "brilliant" and that Marguerite will "love" me.

I don't like this idea of love being tossed around so casually. Love is what Ramie and I have. Love is what Ramie and Jill have. It's not something you dole out indiscriminately to teachers' assistants, no matter how brilliant they are.

As I stand alone on the sidewalk in front of my building, I realize that Ramie is now spending the next five days with someone she might "love" as much as she loves me. By stark and wildly unfair contrast, I'm facing five days alone. I'm no fan of alone. I've done alone, thank you. Four years of it. I thought my alone days were behind me. Ever since my escape from Jill's bedroom, I've seen Ramie every single day. I go to sleep with her at night and wake up with her in the morning. I can't think of anything worse than being alone.

I hug my arms against the cold; then, looking up, I spot my mother staring down at me through my living-room window. I stand corrected. There is something worse than being alone. It's called breakfast with Helen and Richard McTeague.

The urge to run is overpowering. Then Dad comes to the window and mouths the words "Are you all right?".

I hate him. I hate *her.* I hate them both.

But I'm not wearing a coat, and it's freezing out here.

I look up again, and Dad mouths the word "breakfast?"

If I ran, where would I go? I have no money in my pockets. I have no friends. As a final insult, my stomach growls with hunger.

Fine, I think. They can buy me breakfast if they want, but this in no way means I've forgiven them, and it does *not* make us a family.

Since they're paying, I pick the most expensive brunch place I can think of, which, ironically, is housed in an ancient rusty diner car in the shadow of the Williamsburg Bridge. I order the lobster omelet ($22.00), a *large* freshly squeezed orange juice ($6.00), and a double-shot cappuccino ($5.50). I intend to order dessert as well ($7.00–$11.00). And another cappuccino ($5.50).

After ordering, we all sit in silence for a long time, which is fine by me because I have nothing to say to them.

"So Ramie's going to Paris," Dad says finally. "That's a beautiful city."

"She's going to dump me," I say. I look at my mom. "You're welcome for that."

Mom takes a deep, calming-down breath. "Jack, I don't think Ramie's a bad person," she says. "I just think . . ."

"You think she's a, quote, worshipper of chaos."

Mom nods. "Yes, I think I've used those words. But . . ." She takes a calming-down sip of water. "I know this may be hard for you to believe, Jack, but your pain is not my joy."

"It's not?" I say. "Are you sure?"

"What makes you think she's going to dump you?" Dad says in a bold attempt to hijack the conversation.

I shrug. In all honesty, I was being dramatic. But now that he asks, the idea of Ramie dumping me is suddenly tinged with a halo of plausibility.

"Have you been fighting?" Dad asks.

"No," I say. "But . . ." I stop myself. Why would I share any of this with them? What are they going to do about it?

"Go ahead," Dad says. "We used to be young once. Remember, Helen?"

Mom laughs wistfully.

I almost puke at the thought of them being anything other than old and used up. But then I figure if I don't start talking about a subject *I* care about, Dad's bound to make us share our feelings or something.

"She spends a lot of time in the city," I say. "With that Marguerite girl, the one who's taking her to Paris for some stylist job. Apparently Marguerite's been introducing her to people who are 'really doing it,' whatever 'it' is."

Suddenly a vague Jillmemory comes to me. Not something she did, but something she thought. Ramie's outgrowing us.

Us. Not just her. Jill was thinking of both of us.

The waitress comes with our plates, each one brimming with a gigantic omelet.

"Mmm, that smells good," Dad says. "Good choice, Jack."

"Yes," Mom says. "Food we actually *want* to eat."

I'm starving, so I dig in. I've never eaten lobster before. Jill has. She didn't like it. When I get a bite in my mouth, it's like an explosion of flavor. "Oh my God," I say with my mouth full.

"You like it?" Dad says.

I quickly suppress my pleasure and shrug sullenly. "It's all right."

After that, we eat in silence for a while, both of them

making periodic *mmm*'s of approval. I keep rolling over in my head whether there *is* any plausibility to the Ramie dumping me scenario. She seems happy whenever we're together. But now that I think of it, she does get this faraway look sometimes. Jill's seen it too. She doesn't understand it any more than I do.

"Well, this is just delicious," Mom says. She wipes her mouth daintily. "Jack, are you thinking about Ramie?"

"Don't mind-read me," I say.

"I can't help it," she says. "It's part of a mother's tool kit."

The idea of this loveless software program thinking of herself as my mother almost, *almost* steals my appetite. It's down to the stellar nature of the food that I'm able to keep eating.

"Can I tell you something, Jack?" she says.

I shrug.

She puts her fork and knife down. "One of the most important things in any relationship is that both people bring the same number of cards to the table."

"Uh-huh," I say.

"Do you know what I mean by that?"

"No."

She looks at my dad.

"Your mother's right," he says.

I keep eating. If these two think I'm taking *their* word for what constitutes a good relationship, they're even crazier than I thought.

"When I met your mother at UMass," Dad says. "All she did was talk about poetry."

My mom laughs. "Keats," she says. "I had a crush on Keats."

"A dead guy?" I say. "That sounds about right."

Dad, opting to ignore my comment, jumps right in with, "I remember thinking that this beautiful girl was way too smart for me." He taps his head in case I don't know where smartness is located. "I was pre-law," he says. "But I didn't have any *passion* for it. It was just what I studied between keg parties. You know what I mean?"

"I've never been to a keg party," I say.

"They're greatly overrated," Mom says.

"I've never been to a party."

Dad pauses for the briefest of moments to acknowledge my brilliantly timed intrusion of pathos. Then he brushes it neatly aside with a subject-changing, "Anyway." He takes a sip of his coffee. "I didn't want to lose this little gem to some clove cigarette–smoking philosophy major."

"Like Randall Jordan," she says.

They both laugh.

I'm fully prepared to let them both slip away down memory lane while I consume this pornographically delicious lobster omelet, but Mom drags me back into the nostalgia fest by leaning over and whispering, "He was a poet. Very brooding. Big vocabulary."

"He was a tool," Dad says.

The idea of my mother (a) being into poetry and (b) having guys fighting over her strains credulity. Not that I ever thought about my mom as a young person, but if I did, I'd picture a sadist's apprentice.

"The thing is," Dad says, "I knew if I was going to hold on to her"—he gestures toward my mom with this thumb—"I'd have to pony up in the intellect department." Again, a tap to the head. "So you know what I did?"

I shake my head because the catalog of possible atrocities is virtually limitless here.

"I hit the books," he says. "Not just assigned reading either, but extra stuff. The *philosophy* of law. I realized there was something to it too. Something more than a grade point average."

"He was insufferable," Mom says. "He'd go on and on for hours about case studies and Thurgood Marshall."

"I did go a little overboard," he says. "But hey." He looks at me with a face full of pride. "She's Mrs. Richard McTeague now. Not Mrs. Ran-*tool* Jordan." He winks at me because that little play on words just might be the pinnacle of his comedy career.

Mom and Dad spend the next few moments looking at each other with those misty expressions old people get when they think about themselves as young people.

"Thanks," I say. "You've really given me something to think about. Just so I'm clear: I should worship Thurgood Marshall and fall in love with a dead poet?"

Mom inclines her head at me in exactly the same way she does with Jill. Then she picks up her fork and knife and resumes eating. "Cheekbones," she says.

My dad scrunches up his face at this, but I know what she's referring to. And she knows I know.

For a full twenty-seven minutes (I know because I keep checking the clock on my cell phone), we manage to eat and chat without stabbing each other with the cutlery. But it's all too intense for me. It might be easy for Mom, now that the new software has kicked in, to pretend she likes me, but I find the endeavor emotionally grueling. I'm an honest person, a trait Jill ascribes to my inherent simplicity. Call it what you will, I'm against lying, and this make-believe family brunch is a fraud. I'm glad when it's finally over.

Once Mom's paid and we've gone outside, I'm so worried Dad's going to suggest another family outing to prolong the togetherness, I fake a text from an imaginary friend.

"Oh crap," I say. "I'm supposed to meet this guy in, like, an hour."

Mom and Dad look at each other because they don't believe me, which makes sense, since today was supposed to be Jilltime. Luckily, they're decent enough to let it go.

Mom glances at her watch. "Maybe we should head back," she says. "And avoid the weekend traffic."

Dad nods. "It sure was great seeing you, Jack," he says. "I hope you know I mean that."

"Yeah," I say. "I know you do." That's all I'm willing to give him right now.

"Do you need anything?" Mom says. "T-shirts or anything?"

I shake my head.

Mom reaches into her purse and produces a handful of cash. "Jill wanted some boots," she says. "And why don't you get yourself something."

I stare at the wedge of bills. There must be over a hundred dollars.

"It's not a bribe," she says. "You can keep hating me if you want to."

"Promise?"

She nods.

I take the money.

"Can we get a taxi here?" she says. "Our car's in the hotel garage in Manhattan."

I look both ways down the street, but there aren't any taxis. "Yeah, it might take a minute."

Dad looks pleased. "I'm in no hurry."

I scan the street in desperation. About a block and a half away is a car that might be a taxi. The local Williamsburg ones aren't yellow, so it's hard to tell. I step out into the street to flag it down. As it gets closer, however, I realize it's just some guy in a big blue sedan.

"You'll call if you need anything," Mom says. "Right?"

"Sure," I say.

"And tell Jill . . ." She stops and shakes away the thought.

"Tell her what?" I ask.

"Nothing," she says. "Just take care of yourself. That's all."

I nod. Another big dark car approaches the intersection a block away, and I step out into the street to get a better look. I spot the Northside Car Service logo on its side. I wave my arm like a lunatic, and it flashes its lights at me. But it's stuck at a red light.

"This one'll take you," I say.

Mom nods.

"Well, I guess this is it," Dad says. He punches me on the shoulder. "See you around, partner. He pauses for a second, perhaps hoping for a last-minute hug. Out of instinct, I jerk toward him, then back off.

When the light changes, the Northside car makes its way toward us.

"Hey, Mom?" I say.

"Yes?" she says.

It feels strange to say the word "Mom" without sneering. "Jill doesn't want to go to NYU," I tell her. "Or Columbia or Esswich Aggie."

"I figured," she says. "Where does she want to go?"

"Nowhere," I say.

"I don't understand."

"Neither does she," I say.

When the Northside car stops in front of us, I hold up my finger to the driver and he nods.

"It's Tommy Knutson," I tell my mother. "Jill's waiting to see where he ends up."

"Oh," she says. "I thought they broke up."

"They did," I say.

Mom doesn't get it. But then why would she?

"It's kind of a mess in here." I tap my head as reference. "She does things without knowing why. Sometimes she ratio- nalizes them after the fact."

"I see," Mom says.

"She's a sensible girl for the most part," I say. "But some- times . . ." I shake my head.

Mom smiles. "Tell me about it," she says.

"She needs to put Knutson behind her," I say. "Once and for all."

Mom nods. "It's not always easy."

"Yeah," I say. "What ever is?"

Mom and I share a look, then, whose meaning is unclear but which nevertheless brims with honesty. I open the back door to the car and lean in. "They're going to midtown," I tell the driver.

He nods.

My parents get into the car with no further attempts at hugging or meaningful glances, which is a small mercy. As I watch them go, I realize this is the second time in one day that a black car has left me alone on a sidewalk in the cold.

To my great discomfort, I find myself sort of missing them.

What a pair of jerks! They buy me one stinking meal and it upsets everything I thought I knew about them. I've never felt anything but anger toward my parents. It wasn't pretty, but at least it was manageable. I knew the contours and limitations of that anger. I could indulge it safely. What am I supposed to do with *these* feelings? I can't even name them. I'd have to invent words for them.

And what's up with that nostalgia fest about how they met? Am I supposed to relate to them as people now? People who used to be young? Like me? It makes me sick.

With nowhere to go but my empty apartment, I ramble toward the waterfront, eventually winding up at a dirty "park" where a bunch of people around my age smoke cigarettes and drink coffee from paper cups. I hang back and observe them, knowing that none of them will talk to me and not knowing how to talk to them. I haven't yet learned the fine art of making friends, and I'm beginning to suspect it's beyond my abilities. Eventually I walk to the river's edge and stare into the green-brown water of the East River.

What if Mom's right about bringing cards to the table? Am I going to lose Ramie to some clove cigarette–smoking philosophy major? Or worse yet, to some assistant to the assistant to the number three stylist in the industry? I can't just stand by and let that happen. I have to do something to prevent it.

The green-brown water of the East River offers little in the way of inspiration, so I turn my back on it and head home. It seems so obvious now that the only way to hold on to Ramie is to do something with my life. Something interesting. And important. If I'm going to continue qualifying for a girlfriend of Ramie's stature, I need to start bringing some friggin' cards to the table. Because right now I'm not bringing anything.

My pace quickens, and before long, I'm running. It feels good to run. It has direction and purpose. I promise myself that by the time I make it home, I will have some cards for the table. Good ones too. If Jill wants to waste her life waiting to see where Tommy Knutson lands, that's fine for her. But Jack McTeague is going to *be* somebody.

That's right. I'm going to count. People will know my name. When I die, they'll say, "Jack McTeague did that. Oddly, he had no birth certificate. Nevertheless, he did that. He *really* did it."

●

A few minutes later I'm knocking on Natalie's door.

She opens it with a cup of coffee in her hand.

"Hi," I say. "I'm Jill's brother, Jack. I need a job."

She stares at me. "You and Jill have the exact same haircut."

"I know," I say. "I need a job."

"Are you twins?" she says. "Is that a freaky twins thing?"

I nod. "I'll work for free. I'm only here about four, maybe five days a month. But I'll work hard. I promise."

She leans against the doorjamb and regards me appraisingly. "Can you do anything?"

The list of things I can "do" is both limitless and X-rated, but I am not here to prostitute myself. "You have a magazine, right? I can, like, proofread it or something."

"I don't need a proofreader," she says.

"I can type," I say.

"I don't need a typist. Wait here." She closes the door. About ten seconds later she returns and shoves a magazine in my face. "You're eighteen, right? That's my demo. Have a look at my mock-up and tell me if *you* think it's too safe."

I take the magazine and flip through the pages.

"You're bored, right?" she says. "You think it's boring."

"Um, I don't know." I flip through page after page of ads for sunglasses and handbags.

She rips it out of my hands, flips through it, and shows me some fashion type pictures. "Boring, right?" She flips backward to an article about some Brooklyn-based DJ. "See?

Boring." She takes it back. "That's what my investors said. Boring and safe."

"So why don't you fix it?"

"Great idea."

"I can help," I say.

"How?" Natalie's eyes fix on mine.

"I could be a model."

"No you couldn't," she says. "And I don't need a model. What I need is a story. Something controversial. Something completely original. So unless you've got an angle on something groundbreaking, I'm afraid there's little you can do for me." She takes a sip of her coffee while her eyes flick around my face and hair. "It's uncanny," she says.

"What?"

"The resemblance."

"Yeah," I say. "I know."

Later that day, while I'm nursing a pumpkin smoothie at this juice bar in the neighborhood, I realize that Natalie is, unbeknownst to her, living exactly one floor beneath her groundbreaking story. I don't think it's an exaggeration to say that a story about me and Jill could launch a journalist's career. Plus we'd be famous. And rich too, because famous people are rich. Jill could give up her temp job and get invited to A-list parties where she'd eventually meet a rock guitarist or a world-renowned paleontologist who'd help her finally get over Tommy Knutson.

Me? I'd be the desire of every woman in America. But

they'd have to eat their poor little hearts out because I'm a one-woman man. Also, I could tell the whole world about how my mother locked me up. She'd be reviled, globally.

Hmm, that doesn't feel nearly as satisfying as it should.

At any rate, when it comes to fame, there are cons to balance out the pros. There'd be paparazzi and intrusive medical type questions. Nosy reporters would dig through my trash.

Plus, I don't think Jill would appreciate it one bit. In fact, if she ever woke up to find CNN knocking on the door, it would be the end of her. She'd say something on the order of, "I deeply can't be*lieve* Jack spilled our dirty secret when I've tried soooo hard to protect it. Mal!" Then she'd lock herself in the bedroom, stare into the mirror, and marinate in self-pity.

In the end I decide, for her benefit more than my own, that the cons of fame outweigh the pros.

I'll have to rescue Natalie's magazine with a different groundbreaking story. But it occurs to me while I'm slurping my smoothie that I'm not exactly in a position to find a groundbreaking story, or any story at all, since I don't know anyone, don't do anything, and the odds of anything groundbreaking suddenly occurring through the window of this juice bar are vanishingly small.

Eventually, with nothing but the watery dregs left of my pumpkin smoothie, my cell phone beeps. It's a text from Ian Larson. Check this out:

Ur right it was stupid im thru w them and stupid chart cant stop thinking about u

(re)cycler

He can't stop thinking about her? That's an unexpected twist. I had Larson pegged for a skinny creep who spent his weekends scouring the Burg for underage girls. I figured he'd move on to the next tender morsel and forget all about Jill. Is it possible he actually *likes* her?

Oh, who cares? He's still a skinny creep. I'm about to pose as Jill and send him a blistering hate text, when all of a sudden Larson's unexpected Jill-positiveness starts to feel like an opportunity. My mind fizzles. An idea begins to emerge. I suck back the final sip of my pumpkin smoothie and allow the idea to gestate in the fetid swamp waters of my mind. I have a good mind, you see, capable, if nourished properly, of all manner of brilliance.

Here, perhaps, is Natalie's story, sitting right under the bony ass of Ian Larson.

I text him back:

Meet me at the McCarren Park dog run in ten minutes.

Don't worry. I have a plan.

Ten minutes later Larson lopes his way down Driggs Avenue, wearing this giant blue anorak with a matted fur collar that looks like ants live in it. He scans the perimeter of the dog run in search of Jill. The second he recognizes *me*, he stops.

"I'm not going to hurt you," I tell him.

He stays where he is, a good ten feet away. "Where's Jill?" he says.

"Out of town," I say. "Larson, I have a proposal for you."

He doesn't move.

"I don't bite," I tell him. "For crud's sake, Larson, are you going to come over here or am I going to have to yell my proposal to you?"

Reluctantly, he lopes over to where I'm leaning against the dog fence. "Okay," he says. "What do you want?"

"What I want," I say, "is justice."

"What?"

"Dude," I say. "You know who thinks justice is way impressive?"

He shakes his head.

"Jill," I say.

"Really?"

I nod. "It's, like, her number two turn-on."

"What's number one?"

"Don't get ahead of yourself," I say. "Now listen."

Larson's all ears. I seem to have a strange power over him. Although he clearly thinks I'm deranged, he finds it difficult to defy me, as if I exude a natural authority. I make a mental note of this and vow always to use it for good, not ill.

"Here's my plan," I tell him. "You steal the girl-trader chart from your degenerate friends, and Natalie publishes it in her magazine next to a tell-all interview with a former—no, a *reformed* girl-trader, a.k.a. you."

I pause to let him adjust to the glaring genius of it all, but he only looks at me dumbly.

"You see, Larson, it's both a cautionary tale *and* a story of redemption."

"Uh-huh," he says.

"You know who thinks redemption is unbelievably cool?"

"Jill?"

I nod deeply.

"You're nuts," he says.

He starts walking away, but I catch up and plant myself right in his path.

"Larson, I'm trying to help you."

"Why?" he says. "What's in it for you?"

"Me?" I say. "I'm in it for the justice. Don't be so cynical."

Larson does have the cheekbones for cynicism. Maybe that's what Jill liked about him.

"Anyway," I say. "What difference does it make what *I* want? Do it for your own sake. Do it because you know Jill will practically throw herself at your feet for being so . . . courageous. Courage being, I *think*, number four on her list of turn-ons."

"Should you be talking about your sister like this?"

I shrug. "We're all adults here. Look, I'm not saying you should do it *only* for the hero-worship sex. Do it because it's the right thing to do. Think of the hero-worship sex as a fringe benefit."

Larson shifts back and forth on his feet, which gives the impression of a badly constructed high-rise swaying in an earthquake. "You really think she'll dig it?"

"Call her," I say. "See what she says."

With my hand in my pocket, I make sure the volume's turned off on my cell phone; then I stand by innocently while Larson calls Jill and leaves the following Larsonian message:

"Hey, Jill. It's Ian. Um, this is kind of weird, but your brother's trying to get me to, um, steal Perm's chart for justice or something? And I was wondering . . . um . . . what you thought. I'll do it if you think I should. I mean, I guess I kind of owe it to you."

"And to womankind," I whisper.

"And to womankind," he says.

I wink at him.

"So anyway, let me know what you think. Oh and, um, call me if you want to hang out sometime." He hangs up.

"Not sure I would have added the last part," I say. "She hasn't forgiven you yet."

"Shoot," he says.

"It's okay. It's okay. She probably will. I mean, she defo will if you get the chart."

"Defo?"

"British slang," I say. "So, are you in?"

He shrugs. "I'll see what she says."

"Wise man."

He narrows his eyes at me. "So, are you and Jill, like, twins?"

I nod.

"Do you, like, read each other's minds and stuff?"

I lean toward him ominously. "I'm reading her mind right now."

He backs away, but he keeps looking right at me.

"Yup," I say. "She's thinking, I wonder if I should get that voice mail from Ian. He kind of hurt my feelings, what with being a girl-trader and all, but other than that, he seemed nice.

And he was—" I have to suppress the gag reflex when I say this next part. "He was deeply, deeply cute."

"You're so full of shit," Larson says.

"Maybe I am. Maybe I'm not."

He backs off a few steps, then turns and walks away.

"So are you in or what?" I yell.

"I'll let you know," he yells back.

"Well, don't take too long, guy. This clock is ticking."

He shrugs and lopes his bony way down Driggs Avenue.

Now, I know Jill's mind better than my own, but I still can't figure out what she ever found attractive about Larson. To me he looks like the unholy offspring of a skeleton and some garbage. Girls can be so demented.

When he's safely out of view, I text him the following:

Defo snag the chart! I luv it! Justice rules. CU in few days? Xoxo Jill

About ten minutes later Larson texts back:

Will do wont be easy.

What a hero.

The next morning I call Manpower temp agency to tell them that Jill, who was supposed to be working at some insurance company, is deathly ill. I try to keep it vague so as not to permanently ensnare her in any employment-threatening deception. The next thing I do is go downstairs and propose my ingenious Cautionary Tale slash Redemption Story idea to Natalie.

She shoots it down.

"Boys being dogs?" she says. "That's not news."

But when I report that her name is *on* the chart, with two X's (one for Perm and one for Alvarez), she has a complete change of heart.

Her exact words are, "I can't believe that pair of grade-B hamburgers put *my* name on a chart!"

The story's a go. While I'm waiting for Larson to deliver the chart, Natalie phones Perm, Alvarez, and Sasha and tells them she's doing portraits of the "hottest hipsters in Brooklyn," and would they consider posing for her photographer friend. What they don't know is that they are going to be exposed as the girl-trading ass faces they are by being styled in preposterous clothes. Can you even imagine what chubby Sasha is going to look like stuffed into vinyl jeans?

Vinyl jeans.

And the best part of this diabolical plan is that I get to offer the job of styling these unwitting scumholes to my awesomely talented girlfriend. Forget about being the assistant to the assistant. This is a real gig. She's getting a credit for it. Man, she is going to worship me.

So on Thursday afternoon I'm walking home from my favorite Polish meat market with my favorite type of kielbasa when Natalie texts me the following:

> Perm and gang are all go! Shooting Sat. Book Ramie. Wheres effing chart! Dont fail me! Xoxo

It's all down to me now. Or, more specifically, it's down to Larson. Talk about a weak link in the chain. Allegedly, he's not even speaking to the girl-traders anymore. Somehow he has to hot-finger the chart—the *actual* chart—away from them. Natalie was clear on that point. She doesn't want to publish a reproduction. She wants the genuine article, complete with beer stains and finger smudges.

It's day five of my phase, which already makes this a long one. Chances are I'll be gone tomorrow. If Larson doesn't make good on the chart today, the whole project could go kerplewy.

That night, I'm waiting for Ramie to get home from Paris, grateful that I'll get at least one night with her (a night I intend to exploit to the fullest). I've cleaned the apartment, showered, dressed in freshly laundered clothes, and even put some stuff in my hair so it doesn't poke out all over my head. As I sip ginger ale in anticipation of her arrival, it gives me the opportunity to appreciate the multifaceted benevolence of my work. Provided Larson doesn't screw the whole thing up by failing to deliver the chart, I can lay claim not only to saving Natalie's magazine but also to defending womankind *and* getting Ramie a killer assignment. I am, one could argue, a bona fide gift to the women of this world. Women, you're welcome.

When I hear Ramie's keys in the door, I put the ginger ale down and have one quick look at myself in the darkened window. I want to *be* a force of benevolence in the world, but I don't want to look like one. I want to look like a dangerous sexual animal. Which I do. Ramie gets the door open, kicks her suitcase across the threshold, then collapses across it.

"Bed," is all she says.

I rush over, pull her up off the suitcase, and drag her to the couch with me.

"So tired," she says. "So deeply tired."

I try to sit her up, but she's like deadweight. "Rames?" I say.

She looks up at me, smiles sleepily, then nestles her head in my lap and curls up like a cat. The apartment door is still open, having caught on the edge of her suitcase.

"You smell different," I say.

"Stella," she says. "Free sample. Sleeping now."

"Rames," I say. I shake her gently, and she groans. "Ramie, I have some big news for you."

"Uh-huh," she says. She nestles further onto my lap and covers her face with her hand.

"Ramie?"

She groans again. I take a sniff of her new perfume.

"I don't like it," I say.

"Yeah," she says. "It's nice, isn't it?"

"I said I *don't* like it."

"Good night," she says.

I give up and let her sleep on me for about half an hour, then gently slide out from underneath her and drag the suitcase into her room.

About an hour later Ramie wakes up, totally confused, and stumbles to the bathroom. I hear the shower turn on, followed by a scream. When I run inside, Ramie is stepping backward out of the shower.

"It's cold!" she says.

I wrap her in a towel and sit her down on the closed toilet seat.

"Jeeze, Rames," I say. "Did you leave your brain in Paris? It takes a minute for the water to heat up."

Ramie nods with her eyes closed. "Can I have a bath instead?"

"Sure," I say. I run the water for her. "But only if I can watch."

She's too jet-lagged to resist.

Once she slides in, Ramie can do little more than lie back in the tub while I wash her. But after a while she starts to revive.

"Paris," she says. "*Mon dieu!* It was so cool. We shot this muse, named Debra, at the Ritz. Do you know that muse is an actual job? Mal, you would not believe the amount of couture. I mean she actually wears couture. All the time."

I let her talk while my hands wander all over her body under the guise of hygiene. I don't understand anything she's talking about, but I'm not sure this matters. I think she just needs to download it all so she can clear space in her brain. This is good, because I am about to fill her brain with an inspirational tale of my own.

"Marguerite says school doesn't even matter," she says. "Marguerite thinks I should just move to Paris."

"What?"

"Don't worry," she says. "My parents would deeply kill me if I did that." She starts to get out of the tub. I back up and watch her as she dries off. "What are you looking at?" She wraps the towel around herself coyly, then heads into her bedroom. I follow close on her heels. When she opens her underwear drawer, I close it gently.

"Don't bother," I say.

She looks at me.

"When I tell you the amazing thing I have done—not just for you personally, but for the universe as a whole—you won't be able to resist making love to me."

"What are you talking about?" she says.

I take her hand and sit her down on the edge of the bed. Ramie furrows her brow in suspicion.

"What?" I say. "You think you're the only one with stuff to do? I have stuff."

"What stuff?"

"Important stuff," I say.

"Such as?"

"Prepare to be dazzled," I say. Then, as I pace back and forth in front of her, I reveal the whole ingenious plot, including Ramie's part in it all. While I tell my tale, I strip down to my boxer shorts in order to speed things along to the next inevitable step.

"Natalie's going to call the story 'Sleeping with the Enemy,' " I say. "Oh, and she's getting vinyl jeans for Sasha—you know, the chubby guy?"

The chubby guy you thought was cute, I think, but I don't say that aloud.

"So?" I say. "What do you think?"

Ramie remains sitting, her towel wrapped chastely around

her body, her face frozen in an expression I can't quite place. After a prolonged pause, she says, "I can't believe you did that."

"What do you mean?" I say.

She stares in silence for a second. "I don't know what's worse," she says. "The fact that you told Ian Jill would have sex with him if he stole the chart, or—"

"No, no, no," I interrupt. "Ramie, I was *lying* to Larson. I thought I made that clear. Of course Jill's not going to have sex with him. She's completely over him. I was only saying that to motivate him."

"You sent him a text," she says. "That he thinks is from Jill."

"Yeah?" I say. "So?"

"So how do you think Jill is going to feel about that?"

"Well . . ." Truthfully, I didn't even consider this. It was outside the parameters of the project.

Ramie gets up from the bed and whips off her towel. But before I'm able to hope that at last the hero-worship sex is to begin, she starts dressing.

"I don't understand, Ramie. I thought you'd love this."

. She laughs joylessly as she slides her long, delicious legs into some jeans.

"Wait," I say. "Just wait." I grab her wrist.

She freezes for a second as she stares at my hand; then she looks up at me.

"Why are you so mad?" I say. "I didn't think Jill would mind. She's not dating him or anything. It's completely over between them."

Ramie looks down and shakes her head. "It's not just that," she says.

"What is it, then?"

She pulls her wrist free. "Never mind," she says. "You wouldn't understand." She pulls a sweater on and storms out of the room.

I follow her into the living room. "What do you mean I wouldn't understand?"

At the front door, she slides into her coat.

"Where are you going?" I ask.

"Marguerite's."

I press myself into the front door to block her escape. "Ramie," I say. "I don't understand what's going on here. I got you a job. Did you not hear that part?"

Ramie finishes zipping up her coat, then stares at me coldly.

"What?" I say. "Why are you looking at me like that? Did I not get you a job?"

"Yes," she says. "You got me a job *satirizing fashion.*"

"Huh?"

"Thanks a lot," she says. "It warms my heart to know that you have such a high opinion of my work."

She grabs the doorknob and yanks at it, but the weight of my body prevents the door from opening.

"Will you please move? I want to go."

"Where?" I say.

She sighs impatiently. "I already told you. Marguerite's."

"Of course," I say. "Is she your new BFF or something? Are you dumping Jill too?"

"Do you realize how paranoid you sound?"

"I'm just curious," I say. "Is Jill even your best friend anymore? Because it doesn't seem like you appreciate her very much."

"Oh, you're one to talk," she says. "You don't have any idea how much Jill's sacrificed for you."

"Really?" I say. "Oh, that's right. How could I possibly know how much Jill's sacrificed. It's not like *I remember everything*!"

"Your memory is a lot more selective than you realize," she says. "Will you please move?"

"No," I say.

"I'm going to Marguerite's."

"You know, I don't think it's such a great idea for you to be running off to foreign countries with this teacher's assistant. What about your classes? What kind of an example is she setting?"

"What are you, my mother?" she says. "Marguerite is a *working stylist*. Not that this means anything to you, because you obviously think fashion is a joke, which, by the way, is a total cliché and a typically male thing to think."

I back off with my hands raised. "Whoa," I say. "Where did all this come from?"

But Ramie takes the opportunity to open the door and slip through.

"Ramie!" I shout after her.

She runs down the stairs without answering. I'm about to run after her when I realize I'm still in my underwear. I rush back inside and throw on my jeans and sneakers. The buzzer sounds.

I press the button hoping for Ramie, but it's Larson.

"I've got the chart," he says.

I buzz him in, then go to the window and watch Ramie walk off down the sidewalk. I open the window and shout her name, but she doesn't hear me.

When I open the door for Larson, he has this dumb smile on his face. "You would not believe what I had to go through to get this thing," he says. "I can basically never talk to Sasha again."

I take it from him. "Is that a loss?"

He shrugs. "Actually, I was getting kind of sick of him." He looks over my shoulder into the apartment.

"She's not back yet," I say.

He looks dejected.

"Don't worry," I say. "I'll be sure to tell her what a hero you are." I shut the door.

Two seconds later I open it, and he's still standing there, confused.

"Can I ask you a question?" I say.

He nods.

"Why'd you do it?"

"Do what?"

"Steal the chart?"

"Dude," he says. "You asked me to."

"I know," I say. "But did you do it because it's the right thing to do or because you think it'll get you laid?"

Larson stares at me with this wide-eyed look, as if he's expecting me to lunge at him or something.

"I'm just curious," I say. "Don't worry, I won't tell Jill."

He starts backing away. "You are one seriously disturbed brother."

"Hey," I say. "You didn't answer the question."

All I hear is the sound of his lopey footsteps descending the stairs.

Jill

"He promised Ian I'd have sex with him?"

Ramie nods. We're packed like sardines into this ultrahip art opening in some grungy fifth-floor gallery in Chelsea. Ramie's just filled me in on the precise details, as far as she knows them, regarding Jack and Ian's chart-for-sex scheme.

I have to shout because dance music is blaring from another room. "Like, actual *sex*?"

"Yup!" she shouts back. "How much do you remember?"

I awoke this morning with only dim memories of the incidents in question and had no time to meditate, because I was immediately summoned to a law firm in midtown by Trish from Manpower, who kept asking me if I was sure I felt okay.

"Not much!" I shout. "He came five days early! Did you know that?"

She nods.

"He had brunch with my parents!"

"I know!" she says. "You're remembering a lot more now! Aren't you!"

It's not an appropriate venue for discussing anything that can't be shouted one syllable at a time, so Ramie takes my hand and leads me away. I assume she's taking me to a quiet bathroom or hallway, but instead, she leads me *toward* the music to another room, where a throbbing mass of artfully dressed-down people sway and pulse as if they were one giant organism.

"Come on!" she mouths. She clings to my wrist and slices through the crowd. In the center of the mass is a tall, beautiful redhead dancing by herself. Ramie shouts an introduction to Marguerite, then ignores me for the next half hour in order to dance with her.

To avoid feeling like a fool, I sway awkwardly from side to side just behind Ramie. Because I had to come directly from work, I'm still wearing my wage slave uniform, which consists of a boring gray skirt suit and a plain white shirt. I only had time to dash into a cheap accessories store and buy a wide black corset belt. It improves the silhouette somewhat, but I still look like someone's secretary.

Anyway, I didn't come here to dance. I came here to get the details from Ramie on Jack's last phase, details I deeply need. Ramie, however, is committed to losing herself in both the music and the reflected stunningness of her stunning friend Marguerite. They're the stars of the dance floor. Every single guy in the room wants them. Probably some girls too. Not that they care. They're just having fun, which only makes them more starlike.

Slowly, I inch my way out of their halo to the perimeter of

the dance floor to watch them. It must be incredible to have so much sex appeal that you can safely ignore it. I think it's down to confidence. Ramie didn't have to change anything about herself in order to fit in here. She's a beautiful fish in a pond designed for her survival.

If I were a lesser person, I'd be jealous.

That night when I get home, I meditate into Jackspace and uncover most of the details myself. I'm getting very good at it now, for better and worse.

Ramie spends the rest of my phase crashing at Marguerite's. It's just easier, she explains, because it's so close to school. Sometimes I worry that I'm losing Ramie to Marguerite. (Jack worried about this too, which, in a way, is kind of sweet of him.) But I know how important it is for Ramie to get ahead in her career, and I don't want to hold her back.

Don't worry, I'm not "marinating in self-pity" or anything (yes, I dug out that Jackthought). With Ramie gone, the apartment has never been cleaner. Plus, without much in the way of a social life, I can work a lot of overtime, which, at time and a half, is fattening up my bank account quite nicely. The extra discretionary cash, when combined with the money my mom left with Jack, has allowed me to buy not only those boots I've been lusting after, but also a sexy new pencil skirt to go with them. Perfect for a date, should such an event occur.

All in all, I'm embracing Ramie's absence because it allows me to embark on a new chapter in my life, a chapter I have entitled "Dealing with Stuff in a Solo Type Fashion Because Your BFF Has Other Stuff to Do."

I have elected *not* to deal with the fact that my cycles are getting more and more irregular all the time. Not because it's acceptable to me, but rather because there is not a single thing I can do about it. There is no point in obsessing over things you can't change, a lesson I have learned over the years.

Nor have I elected to deal with the recklessness and stupidity of Jack's behavior vis-à-vis Ian. Reckless and Stupid are Jack's patron saints. Without their guidance, I'm not sure he'd ever do anything. But I can't be too mad at him. He meant well. His sin is one of ignorance, not malice. In fact, the more I get to know Jack, the more I realize that in some ways, his weaknesses are identical to his strengths. He's only able to embark on bold and reckless acts of bravado because he doesn't know any better. I wonder what he'll be like when he does.

At any rate, the thing I *have* elected to deal with, the thing that keeps me up at night, in fact, is Ian himself. He keeps texting and leaving messages, and I have to admit that just knowing there's a boy out there actively wanting to have sex with me is deeply distracting. And the fact that he *stole* something to win my affections is one of the most ego-positive things that's ever happened to me. Stealing is a crime.

Don't get me wrong. Technically, I am morally outraged by the whole thing. I can forgive Jack because he's Jack. But Ian, presumably, did not spend his formative years locked in a room. He's socialized. Shouldn't he know better than to transact for sex with the brother of one's intended? That's, like, gross beyond measure. Right?

Oh, I don't know. Maybe it's not gross. I'm out of my depth here. This is advanced adult sexuality. I haven't even *really* done adolescent sexuality. I'm skipping a whole step. I deeply want to be sophisticated enough to wade through this moral quagmire on my own, but for crud's sake, I'm still a virgin. Is it even safe to wade in alone? I don't want to end up as a cautionary tale.

Ramie's not much help. Mostly through texts and a few rushed coffees at the Starbucks near FIT she advises me to trust my instincts. She keeps mentioning the "tower of Babylon," by which I think she's referring to my virginity. Reading between the lines, I surmise that Ramie is of the opinion that I should stop thinking so much, have sex with Ian already, and get over myself.

She can be so simplistic sometimes. I don't want to pick a fight with her, though, because (a) I'd have trouble scheduling one with her, and (b) I don't want to risk pushing her away for good. For better or worse, Ramie's still my BFF. I'm hoping that the shine will wear off of the stunning and "brilliant" Marguerite eventually and she'll come back down to earth where she belongs. Actually, I'm hoping this for Jack's sake as much as for my own.

So anyway, for two weeks I stew in indecision, deleting Ian's texts without responding. Then, when I realize I'm getting nowhere on my own, I send for reinforcements. I call upon someone with experience, someone who has, by her own admission—and I think this is a direct quote—"had the naïveté screwed right out" of her.

Natalie.

We meet for mushroom pizza at the good place with the mean lady. I'm buying.

After securing a quiet booth in the back, away from both the drunk in the corner and the mean lady behind the counter who has, with great reluctance, given us our pizza and sodas, Natalie gets right down to the business of eviscerating *my* innocence with gritty tales of how she lost her own.

The pageant of sex and debauchery she presents for my education is shocking. I won't abuse your sensibilities with the full details, but rest assured, tears were shed, wisdom gained, pride swallowed. Once, this guy named Brett stole her wallet when she refused to give him a b.j. He justified said action by claiming it was "false advertising" for her to let him pay for dinner, and he was merely getting a refund.

The weirdest thing about that story (and believe me, there are stories far worse) is that Natalie concluded, after the shock wore off, that he sort of had a point.

"I did let him pay for dinner," she says. "I didn't even pretend to reach for the check."

My inability to comprehend any part of this twisted tale is, according to Natalie, damning evidence that I am operating under a "naïve paradigm," which I should reconsider if I'm going to have any success operating in the treacherous waters of the New York dating scene. When I protest that the world can't possibly be as brutish as she describes, she reminds me that we've met today to discuss a guy who, until recently, used to trade girls with his friends.

I can't argue with her on that point.

"So I shouldn't see him?" I ask.

"Do you *want* to see him?"

"Well, yeah," I tell her. "But I don't want to feel like he's *purchased* me."

Natalie sighs, then sips her soda with the vaguely jaded expression of someone who has clearly earned her wisdom. Then she unspools this whole complicated theory about how, in the end, sex is nothing more than a commodity for which everyone barters. When I tell her I'm pretty sure I've never bartered for anything, she tells me this is because I *am* the commodity. You see, I have something Ian wants, and I am "inflating its value" through the economic tactic of "false scarcity." It's like OPEC, she explains, when they withhold oil. For a second I get lost in this metaphor and ask Natalie if I'm the oil. But she says no. I'm Saudi Arabia. The precious commodity I'm hoarding behind my Victoria's Secrets is the oil. She says girls like me are *always* hoarding. We drive guys crazy because we're willing to repress our own sex drives in order to make them want us even more. She used to do it as well. She didn't even know she was doing it.

I confess, neither did I.

"What you have to ask yourself, Jill, is what are you really after? What's the commodity you want?"

I don't have an answer, because I have not been operating under the Commodity Paradigm. There's something ugly and mechanistic about it. It's not far off, in fact, from my mother's approach. They both see men as consumers to be manipulated, which is pretty cynical. And as we all know, I do not have the cheekbones for cynicism.

My instincts, which according to Ramie I should be trusting, tell me to reject Natalie's theory. But then I realize *my* instincts were honed by the dating pool of Winterhead, Massachusetts. I'm not in Winterhead anymore. In fact, the longer I'm away, the more Winterhead seems like a make-believe place. Its tidy rules and quaint values are of no use in these shark-infested waters. If I'm going to thrive here, I may have to acquire some new values, even if those values feel wrong.

Natalie polishes off her second slice of pizza, then takes a big sip of soda. "So is your brother still dating Ramie?" she asks.

"Yes," I say with surprising insistence. "Why?"

She shakes her head. "No reason."

I stare at her for a second, then return to my pizza. I can only hope that Natalie has not set her sights on Jack as her next "commodity." That's the last thing I need.

I spend the next few days pondering Natalie's theory and trying to figure out which commodity I'm after. Love, sex, crude oil? Ramie, who's still crashing at Marguerite's while they work on some massive extracurricular styling project together, weighs in on the matter with the following pithy text:

I think u jus wanna bask in knowldg that someone wants u. don't beat urself up tho. Every 1 wants 2 b wanted. Go 4 it. And send deets!

It takes me a while to figure out whether I should be insulted by that text. In the end, I decide not to be. But I'm still not ready to "go 4 it." It's not that simple, no matter how much Ramie insists that it is.

Now, while I'm trying to solve this highly complex problem, another complex problem resurfaces, courtesy of the reigning Poet Laureate of the Open Road, Tommy Knutson. It's been nineteen days since his last text. Are you ready? Is your haiku translation device turned on? Here it is:

Got mercy?

As if life weren't bewildering enough.

I would very much like to report that I deleted Tommy's text-haiku, gave it no further thought, and went straight back to pondering Ian. But that would be a lie. It turns out I *am* capable of obsessing over two boys at once. A first for me. My vacation from boy obsession is officially over. I do not feel refreshed.

Sadly, I lack the literary talent to deconstruct "got mercy," despite spending two full days on it. You'd be surprised how much potential meaning you can pry out of the word "got."

My opinion on the subject and on all things Tommy-related is thus:

If Tommy Knutson has something to say to me, he should say it in plain English. Until such time as he says stuff in plain English, I shall not respond to any of his texts. I am cutting the cord.

There, I said it. You can't stop me.

Cord cut.

On to the Ian affair.

Ian, unlike a certain other boy, uses normal words like "Um, hi, Jill. Sorry to keep bugging you. Um, I was wondering if you wanted to come over to my place on Friday for, like, dinner? My roommates are out of town for the weekend so . . . um . . . Anyway, you're not, like, a vegan or anything, right? Call me."

I may be operating under a naïve paradigm, but believe me, I know what "like, dinner" means. Ian is not "withholding" anything. His commodity is right out there in the open. It's in the bargain bin.

But do I want it?

I fall asleep that night drowning in indecision and hoping the correct answer will come to me in a dream.

Unfortunately, it doesn't, so the next day, while I'm standing in the shower trying to force myself into a decision, I realize that what's holding me back is my stupid virginity. Natalie's right. I *have* been hoarding. I've been so caught up in losing my virginity at exactly the right time under exactly the right circumstances that I can't even make a simple dinner date with a guy I'm attracted to. My virginity has ballooned all out of proportion.

When I get out of the shower, I make a bold decision. I call Ian and say yes.

And I don't just mean for dinner.

Friday night. Seven p.m. In one hour I will have crossed over into the treacherous world of adult sexuality. Don't try to stop me. I know what I'm doing.

Sort of.

I get through seven different outfits before settling on the following:

- Tight black pencil skirt (for subtle sophistication)
- High black boots (a touch of danger?)
- White ruffled blouse with pointy shoulders (current but playful, not trying too hard)
- Pink bustier just barely visible under the blouse (for maximum devastation)

Ramie's not around, so I take a picture of myself in her full-length mirror and text it to her along with the following:

am losing virginity in this outfit. What do u thnk?

She doesn't respond. Maybe she's on the subway. I send the same image to Natalie, and she calls back with a thumbs-up and tells me to stay cool, make sure he wears a condom, and, no matter how brimming with emotion I may be, avoid at all costs blurting out "I love you."

When we hang up, I look at myself in Ramie's mirror one last time, then turn to the one-armed mannequin. "This is it," I tell her. "I leave here a girl and return a woman."

She doesn't respond. She's clearly been through a lot.

As I'm making my way down Driggs Avenue in the cold, I'm exhilarated by what lies ahead and terrified of messing it up. I have elected to take only one lesson from Natalie's confusing dissertation on the economics of sex. Forget about Saudi Arabia, false scarcity, and bartering. What it comes down to is this:

sex *is* a transaction. It's a transaction of sex. You give sex and you get sex back. That's all. The mistake I've been making is that I've larded the whole enterprise up with love stuff. But love stuff only confuses things. I'm not saying sex and love aren't related. They're cousins. Siblings maybe. But you have to be able to separate them in order to make correct decisions. This is what I got wrong with Tommy Knutson. I was so busy thinking about love, I couldn't do the sex part.

The other thing I got wrong with Tommy Knutson is that I waited too long to *make* the decision. You have to make the decision *before* the moment arrives. Once the moment arrives, your brain is so flooded with sex chemicals and love stuff it's impossible to think clearly. You don't send a soldier into battle and tell her to decide what to do once the enemy starts shooting. You send her in with marching orders. Well, I've given myself marching orders tonight. So now when the enemy starts shooting, I'll know exactly what to do. I won't have to decide anything. The decision has already been made. Brilliant, right?

Thank goodness I've finally seen the light. My virginity is going to slide right off of me. Believe it or not, I used to think of my virginity as something to guard, like a precious gem that evil boys wanted to steal. I think I got that idea from my mother, which is odd, because she never actually said those things to me. She implied them, though.

It seems so silly now, so backward. Virginity is not a badge of honor. If anything, it feels like a badge of dishonor, a constant reminder of my failings with Tommy Knutson. The longer it sticks around, the bigger and uglier it gets.

But tonight I'm going to dispense with it once and for all. Hopefully, once it's gone, I'll be able to think more clearly. I need all the clarity I can get as I continue on my path to becoming Amazing and Wonderful.

Because honestly? Right now? All I am is a virgin.

When Ian opens his door, I can hear quiet guitar music playing.

"Wow! You cut your hair," he says.

I'd forgotten. He hasn't seen me since I ditched the wig. I wonder if he thinks I look too much like Jack.

"Do you like it?" I tug on the ends of it nervously.

"It's awesome," he says. "Come on in." He takes my coat and hangs it on a hook by the door. His eyes linger on mine for a second, then descend downward to take in the full view. His expression is hard to read. I can't tell if he's impressed or disappointed.

"Nice place," I say.

He looks around his apartment. It's bigger than mine but not as neat. It looks like he tidied up, but there are still dust bunnies here and there. In the center of the room is a Ping-Pong table.

"Beer pong," he explains. Then he stares at me for a few seconds. "Sorry," he says. "But you look really hot."

"I do?"

He nods. "Sort of like . . ."

"Like what?" I say.

He shakes his head shyly. "Nothing. But you look good."

"Thanks." I pull a bottle of red wine from my bag and hand it to him. "Natalie recommended it. I don't know anything about wine."

"Me neither," he says.

He takes the wine into the kitchen, which is just a row of appliances against one wall. He stirs something in a pot. "I hope you like beef Stroganoff," he says. "It's the only thing I know how to make." He doesn't look very natural in the kitchen. It's safe to surmise that under normal circumstances, this is a strictly take-out establishment. I do appreciate the effort he's making. But then I can't help but wonder if the whole dinner is a second payment on my body.

After shaking that thought free, I vow to avoid thinking about anything abstract or economic for the rest of the evening. I've already made my decision. All I have to do now is execute.

Ian comes over with two glasses of wine, and we clink them together. I take a small sip. I do not intend to get drunk tonight, because I don't want to lose my virginity in a drunken haze. That would be cowardly, and I am not a coward. Ian keeps his eyes glued to mine.

"You're staring," I say.

"I know. Does that bother you?"

"Would it bother you?"

"No way," he says. "You can stare at me all night if you want. My roommates aren't coming back until Sunday. You can stare at me all weekend."

"Tempting," I say. I sit on the couch and let the tiniest bit of wine moisten my lips. The apartment fills with the warm, rich smell of beef Stroganoff.

"Are you hungry?"

I nod.

●

All through dinner Ian makes heroic efforts to entertain me. He tells me about his run-in with some indie film actor who was shooting something on his block. He tells me how beautiful I am and how much he likes me with short hair. And he keeps refilling my wineglass. I take only small sips, but somehow, by the time we're eating a store-bought chocolate cake, I'm a little tipsy. I guess when someone keeps refilling your glass after every other sip, it adds up.

I tell myself this is okay. I'm not drunk enough to go stumbling around the apartment or puking on his shoes. Perhaps being ever so slightly non-sober will smooth out the edges of my nervousness about losing my virginity.

Not that I want to focus on the momentousness of *that*.

When I fumble slightly on my way to the couch, Ian comes over with his own wineglass and sits right next to me. Then he stares at me full on. He's not nervous anymore. He's determined.

Before I know it, we're kissing. Deep, wet, powerful kisses. Ian guides me gently down on the couch and lies on top of me. Lifting my hands over my head, he begins unbuttoning my shirt.

Very softly, he whispers, "Are you going to say yes to me tonight?"

"Um," I say. "What's the question?"

He opens my shirt and stares at my pink lace bustier. "The question . . . ," he says. His mouth drops open, which is exactly the effect I was aiming for with this thing.

But then, all at once, he pushes my bustier up and, in a forceful yank, peels both it and my shirt clean off!

I swallow.

His eyes adhere with magnetic force to my chest.

"God, you're hot," he says.

"Really?"

He nods, still mesmerized. Then his hands slide under the small of my back. "I don't want to pressure you or anything, but . . ." He fumbles for the clasp to my skirt.

"But what?"

He opens the clasp and pulls the zipper down, his hand getting stuck halfway. It's up to me now. I can either raise my hips to help him unzip my skirt or lie there pressing my butt into the couch to prevent further progress.

It's all on me.

Suddenly an unwelcome cluster of economic concepts start dancing around in my head (false scarcity, bartering, the price of oil). I try to repress them, but this only brings to life a confounding miasma of love stuff. (Is this a relationship? Is Ian the one? Am I still in love with Tommy Knutson?) I'm thinking too much. I've lost the ability to act. My virginity grows by the second. Before long it will become life-size, gain sentience, and sit like a disgusted chaperone on the edge of the couch.

I must take control!

With an enormous force of will, I evict everything from my mind, improvising a new mantra on the spot: *I am a sex machine.* I focus on Ian's body, the weight of it, the length of it.

Before long I am back in the moment, sex chemicals flowing, love stuff extinguished. Clarity regained.

I press my heels into the couch, which frees up my hips. Ian lunges at the gesture by yanking my zipper all the way down. Without wasting any time, he drags the skirt down over my hips. Then he slides off the end of the couch, pulls it all the way off, and throws it decisively on the floor. The only thing separating my precious commodity from Ian's hungry, determined eyes is a pair of pink lace panties.

Ian expresses his appreciation for what he sees by saying something like "Phwoor."

In response, my body tingles with warm, sparkly bubbles of joy.

Ian's about to climb back on top of me when he stops suddenly. "Wait," he says. "Stand up."

"What?"

He backs away from me. "Stand up. I want to see you."

I sit upright on the couch, suddenly embarrassed by my exposed breasts and the way my stomach wrinkles in on itself. I stand up, more out of a desire to present him with a flat stomach than anything else. Ian backs up all the way to the kitchen counter and looks at me. All I'm wearing are my pink lace panties and my high black boots.

"Do you even know how hot you are?" he says.

I can see a warped reflection of myself in the dirty glass door of his microwave oven. I wouldn't say I look beautiful. It's still strange to see myself with short hair. I look so much like Jack in that picture on Ramie's camera. All of a sudden I feel guilty for the memories I'm about to create for him.

I drop my eyes to the floor, thinking, though with less conviction, *I am a sex machine.* Ian picks up both of our wineglasses and gestures toward the bedroom with a head bob. "Come on," he says.

Resisting the urge to cover my breasts, I follow him into the bedroom.

Once there, I try to focus on the details. A bed, a desk, stacks of books, a laptop, one of those collapsible laundry thingies. Ian puts one of the wineglasses on his desk, then turns on a light clipped to the headboard of his bed. He angles it upward so that it casts a warm yellow glow in the room.

I'm pretty sure Ian has done this before, so I can deeply piggyback on his expertise. As long as I don't blurt out "I love you," I'll be fine.

Ian sits on the edge of his bed and has a big sip of wine. "Take your panties off," he says. But it's more of a suggestion than a command. More like, "Hey, here's an idea: Why don't you take your panties off. Might be fun. You know. No big whoop."

When I don't move to take them off, he shrugs. Then he puts his wineglass down and lays back against the headboard with his arms behind his head.

"Am I supposed to be the floor show?" I ask.

"Do you want to be the floor show?" He looks almost hopeful.

I glance up to the ceiling. "I don't think I want to be the floor show."

"Okay," he says. "You could take them off because it's kind of hot in here. It *is* kind of hot in here, right?"

"Not really."

He laughs. "Um, you could take them off because you know how badly I want to see you naked."

"I could," I say.

I *do* like the way Ian looks at me. Once all the complicating abstractions are removed, it's kind of beautiful. There's no mysterious design to it, no hidden motives. He wants me. Plain and simple. There's an animal purity to it.

I start to slide the waistband of my panties downward, keenly aware of how inappropriate it feels to be wearing boots through it all. There's something wrong and thrilling about it. Ian's breathing intensifies as I hesitate, my thumbs just under the waistband. His hunger for me is as naked as I am about to be.

Hmm.

I stop and keep my panties right where they are.

Ian furrows his brow in protest.

"You first," I say.

"What?" he says.

"Stand up," I say.

He laughs dismissively, then sees that I'm serious. "Really?" I nod.

Ian stands up and nervously shoves his hands in the front pockets of his jeans.

"Take your jeans off," I say.

He takes a deep breath and looks at me like he cannot *believe* the nerve I have.

But I'm only finishing what he started.

"I'm serious," I say. "Do it because it's hot in here."

Ian smirks, then commits to the idea and kicks his shoes off. Unbuttoning his jeans very slowly, he pulls them down, revealing white socks and black boxer briefs that are—how shall I put this—anything but flat.

"Keep going," I say.

Ian's expression teeters between outrage and embarrassment. He must be as keenly aware of his bulging erection as I am.

This is fun.

"I'm waiting," I say.

He peels off his socks, then slowly, hesitantly pulls down his boxer briefs.

And there he is, ladies and gentlemen, a man in all his glory.

Out of a sense of decorum, I lift my eyes to his excited and slightly offended face. But they won't stay there. They are pulled, as if by magnetic force, downward.

To his erect thing.

It's not the first time I've seen one. I've seen Tommy Knutson's. I saw Ricky Portland's in sixth grade when he flashed me and Tara Kowalski by the jungle gym. But I've never had one staring back at me so bluntly, at once terrifying and terrified. The things I could do to him right now. Oh, and the things he could do to me.

Ian walks toward me, eyes fixed on mine. When he stands before me, he places his hands on my hips and rips off my panties in one go. Crouching down, he pulls them to my ankles, then drops to his knees and kisses my stomach.

Do you want to know something?

I *am* a sex machine. Not only is my body executing brilliantly, my brain is joined to the task. There is no love stuff mucking up the works. It's all pure sex. No abstractions, just concrete carnality.

The feelings I have for Ian are immediate and physical. I love the mechanics of his body, the logic of the bones and the curve and swell of his muscles. Just look at the way his shoulders move while he inches his lips down my stomach to my hips. He's sinewy where I'm round, angular where I'm curved. We are perfectly matched sex machines, and tonight that is enough. Tonight, that is all that matters. I don't care what any of this *means*. I don't care what happens in the morning. All I want is to surrender to the moment, to disappear into the now. It might be the first time I've ever felt this way. And it feels—sorry, Jack, I know you disagree with this sentiment— freeing.

Ian unzips my boots, and I step out of them. Then he reaches up, grabs my elbow, and pulls me to my knees. We wrap our arms around each other and kiss. His body slides against mine, and before I know it, I am on my back on the scratchy carpet.

We're both naked. The moment is at hand. Before long my virginity, that stupid "tower of Babylon," will be a memory.

"Say yes," he says.

But I don't want to say yes. I don't want to say anything.

He kisses my neck. "Say it," he says. "Say yes."

"Why?" I ask.

His lips wander downward to my breasts. "I need to hear you say it."

But why do we need language? Why can't we let our bodies do the talking? Our bodies know what they want. Look at me. I'm completely naked. I am lying beneath him. I am running my hands up and down his spine. Isn't that enough?

Ian adjusts my legs and positions himself right above me.

"Condom," I say.

"Right." He stretches for one on a milk crate next to his bed. Then he sits up on top of me and opens the package.

I watch him fumble with it, thrilled by the sinewy grace of his body, by the shadow that falls in the hollow above his collarbone. I feel preemptively victorious, already basking in the glory of this momentous thing about to transpire. I'm no longer afraid of its bigness. I'm big enough for it.

As he struggles with the condom package, a vaguely familiar wave builds up from the base of my spine. At first I think I'm having an orgasm, but Ian isn't even touching me.

And I'm not sure what an orgasm feels like.

Suddenly my back arches. Ian stops fiddling with the condom and looks at me, surprised. Then, with a knowing smile, he drops the condom and touches me again. My spine convulses.

"I love the way you do that," he says.

"Stop," I say.

"Why?" he says. "Don't you like it?"

A sharp pain tears through my torso.

"Oh mal," I say.

My hand inadvertently grips the condom.

"It's okay," he says. "We can use that later." He pushes the condom away and tries to touch me.

"No!" I tear his hands away and slide out from under him.

"What's wrong?"

My right arm starts to shake.

"Are you okay?" he asks.

I grab my panties, but they're all twisted up into a ball.

"What's wrong?" he says.

My face grows hot, my vision blurred. I can't untangle my panties. Getting to my feet, I stumble through the door and into the living room.

"Where are you going?" he says.

"Stay away," I tell him.

But he follows me. "Did I hurt you?" he asks.

"No." I grab my coat and slide into it. "Where are my boots?"

"But you can't leave like that," he says.

I push past him into the bedroom and grab my boots. When I rush back, he's standing by the front door, naked.

"What's going on?" he says.

My muscles spasm, and I double over at his feet. He drops to the floor. "Should I call 911?"

I'm panting now. "No," I say. "I have to get home." Using what's left of my strength, I push him away and fumble the door open.

"Wait!" he says.

I rush into the hallway and run down the stairs, gripping my boots in one hand.

When I get outside, the cold smacks me in the face. I'm about half a mile from home. I hear Ian coming down the stairs, so I start running toward Bedford Avenue. Halfway there, my knees give out on me. When I look up, I see Ian running toward me in jeans and his coat but no shirt.

Pulling myself to my feet, I force myself to run. My legs scream at me as the muscles pull and tear. Behind me, Ian is gaining. I have to lose him somehow.

And I have to get home.

I turn left down Bedford Avenue and sprint for the next street. Ian is only half a block behind me. The pain will worsen, and I know I won't be able to run for long. Already my legs are lengthening. I turn left down a quiet street with no pedestrians at all. But I know Ian will catch up with me. Any second now he'll turn down this street. With no place to hide, I hurl myself behind some garbage cans in front of a tenement building. Then I squelch my panting and wait for the sound of Ian's feet.

"Jill!" he calls out.

But he runs right past me.

I pull the coat tightly around me, but my legs are fully ex-posed. Exposed and changing right before my eyes. The pain is unbearable, and I want to cry out.

"Please make it stop," I whisper. "Please oh please oh please."

I tell myself the pain will end. It always does. It comes on like a steamroller, tears me apart, then evaporates suddenly. It always does, and this time will be no different.

Ian runs back in the other direction, calling my name, frantic.

I curl into a ball and grip my stomach. My shoulders bulge and stretch, straining the fabric of the coat until I can no longer keep it closed around me.

Down below, a terrible throbbing begins.

Hold on, I tell myself. It will all be over soon.

What was once a center of softness and exquisite pleasure is now an angry nubbin throbbing to be born.

I bite down hard on the sleeve of my coat and grunt through the agony.

And from somewhere close by is a high-pitched sound.

Insistent and deafening, it must be . . .

november 17

●

Jack

. . . the cell phone?

Where am I?

It's freezing. And I'm wearing Jill's coat.

Ow!

Hold on. I think I'm having a girlgasm.

Wait.

Wait.

Nope.

Just . . . searing . . . pain.

The cell phone chirps at me, so I shove my hand into the pocket of this stupid coat and shut it off. The back of my hand scrapes against the sidewalk.

The sidewalk?

Where the heckfire am I?

Looking up between two trash cans, I spot a pair of dirty Converse sneakers facing me, unlaced. Extending my gaze further upward, I see two long legs and a big blue anorak.

"Jill?" the coat says. "What are you doing?"

It's Larson, and he's squinting into the dark at me.

"Go away," I say.

Ian steps up to the trash cans and peers down at me. "What's wrong with your voice?"

I avert my face as the pain drifts away and evaporates like steam. Reaching down to my crotch, I make sure I'm all there.

Ian hovers over the trash cans to look down at me. "Is there some reason why you're lying there?" he says. "Do you need to go to the hospital . . . or anything?"

I flip onto my other side and put my back to him, hoping that if I play possum, he'll give up and walk away. But instead, I hear him shift one of the trash cans and squeeze through. Then his hand is on my shoulder.

"It's freezing out here," he says. "At least come back inside. I promise I won't touch you. If you don't want me to."

"Go away," I whisper.

"I don't understand," he says. "What did I do? What's wrong?"

He puts his hand on my head. I want to throw him off and stuff his bony ass into a trash can. I want to punch him for the disgusting things he did to Jill. Doesn't he know she's only eighteen? Doesn't he know she's in love with someone else?

"Can you look at me?" he says. "I want to help you."

I take a deep breath and try to summon every ounce of energy I have left. If I'm quick, I can probably knock him down and make a break for it before he sees my face.

Larson tugs me around to face him. "Please," he says. "Just tell me what I can do. Tell me what's . . ."

Once he registers the details of my face, he stumbles backward against the trash cans. "What the hell?" he says.

I climb over him and shuffle down the street. Jill's coat stops midway down my thighs and I'm not wearing anything underneath. I'm still too weak to run, so I throw myself into an awkward speedwalk. I'm barefoot, and the sidewalk is so cold it stings my feet.

Behind me, the trash cans clatter, then Larson's footsteps gain.

"Jack!" he says.

I try to hurl myself into a run, but it's all I can do to maintain verticality and forward motion. I stick to the speedwalk, committing my shoulders and upper body to the task. Two girls walking toward me stop and stare at me openmouthed as I grind past them.

"Jack!" Larson says. "Wait!"

I try to summon the strength from somewhere, anywhere, to move faster, but I've got nothing. Larson catches up to me easily, grabs me by the arm, and spins me around.

"What's going on?" he says. "Where's Jill?"

I bend over and rest my hands on my knees to try to catch my breath. "I don't know," I say.

"But you're wearing her coat."

"Yes. I know." I look up at him. "And you put your dirty hands all over her! You . . . you . . . you heap of garbage!"

I storm off, panting and exhausted, but determined to get away.

Bedford Avenue lies ahead, its sidewalks heaving with the Friday night masses. I put my head down and charge right out there. I do not make eye contact with anyone, though it's clear from the hurried parting of shoes on the sidewalk that my presence is noticed.

"Jack!" Larson yells from somewhere behind me. "Wait!"

I sneak a peek at him over my shoulder. Then I charge right into the slow-moving traffic and cross the street to the improvised bebop of car horns and curses. On the opposite sidewalk, a crush of smokers banished to the curbside see me coming and scatter.

Larson follows right on my heels, eventually grabbing me with both hands and spinning me around. "What have you done with her?" he says.

I'm too weak to resist. My last watt of power was expended making it across the street. "Larson," I say between hoarse breaths. "Believe me . . . you are not . . . in a position . . . to understand. . . . Just . . . let it go, okay?"

"Let what go?"

I stare at the ground for a few seconds, waiting for my strength to return.

"Let what go?" he says, as if I didn't hear him the first time.

I look up into his big, stupid face. Is it pity? Is that what she sees in him? Because whatever it is, I can't see it. He's not attractive. He's not smart. He's not charming or funny. He's no Tommy Knutson, that's for sure.

For a second I'm tempted to tell Larson the truth about Jill and me. I'm pretty sure that would put an end to the affair. But I guess it's not my affair to end, no matter how disgusting and wrong it is.

"Larson," I say. "Don't ask questions you don't want the answer to."

"Huh?"

I punch him collegially on the shoulder and speedwalk away.

At last my strength returns. I start to jog, then to run.

"Wait!" he calls.

But he chases me for only a few blocks. By the time I get to McCarren Park, he's gone.

I run close to the wrought-iron gate enclosing the park, beneath the archway of nude maple branches. The dwindling pedestrians I encounter skirt away of their own accord. There is however a brief chorus of appreciation, courtesy of some drunks who haunt one of the benches on the outskirts of the park.

About a block away from home I realize I've left Jill's boots behind those trash cans. They were expensive too. By the time I drag myself up the stairs and inside the apartment, I'm completely out of breath.

"Ramie!" I gasp.

I collapse on the sofa and wriggle out of Jill's coat.

"Ramie, are you here?"

She's not. She's at Marguerite's in "the city," where she always is nowadays. I pull the cell phone out of Jill's coat pocket and call her, but she doesn't answer.

Lying on the couch, I try to evict the sense memory of Jill's near deflowering, but I'm not so good at repression. That's a Jill skill. For me, the sensation of Larson's thing so close to hers is as crisp and vibrant as the pain in my lungs from all that running.

To add insult to injury, I'm hatching a boner. I stand up and try to walk it off, but it won't go away. Giving in, I lie down on Ramie's bed and dredge up vivid memories of the last time we had sex. But this only reminds me that I hardly saw her at all last phase. My most vivid memory is of her running down the stairs after our fight. After a few minutes, the Viking deflates. It's almost a relief.

Exhaustion reappears, and I fall asleep in Ramie's bed.

The next morning, the cell phone chirps me awake with a text from Ramie.

OMG! Did u do it?

I call her back immediately, but she tells me she can't talk because she's doing "pickups" for another assistant-to-the-assistant gig with Marguerite. When I tell her I absolutely *must* see her, she sighs in frustration, then gives me Marguerite's address, along with the warning that she swears to God she can only spare, like two seconds.

I shower quickly to wash off the residue of Larson, then throw on a clean T-shirt and jeans, grab my coat, and run to the subway. Marguerite's apartment is a block away from the FIT campus in a fancy brownstone from another century. Marguerite opens the door.

"You're?" she says.

"Jack," I say.

She keeps staring.

"Ramie's boyfriend?" I say.

She nods slowly as the concept begins to make sense to her. "Oh yeah," she says. "Jill's brother, right? Jack McGee?"

"McTeague."

"Of course," she says. "Come in."

She leads me into a gaping entrance hall, which is almost as beautiful as she is.

I hate that she's so beautiful.

"It's ridiculous, isn't it?" she says. "This town house was my great-grandmother's. My family has always had a great affinity for New York. The English can be like that, you know."

"Uh-huh," I say.

She leads me farther inside to an old-fashioned drawing room with wood-paneled walls, a baby grand piano, and a humongous chandelier. She's right. It *is* ridiculous. My mother would love it. Class and old money everywhere, but all of it casually tarnished as if it didn't matter so much. Every surface is draped with clothes and plastic hanging bags for clothes. Marguerite has turned this palace into a workspace.

"Ramie's gone," she says. "You just missed her." She picks up two sequined dresses by the hangers and lays them across a pile of other dresses on top of the piano.

"It's okay," I tell her. "I can wait."

Her eyes flick to mine for a second; then she searches around the room. "She's not coming back." She stalks over to a wingback chair, picks up a black velvet jacket by the hanger, and lays it across the other clothes on the piano. "She's at a showroom." She searches around the room for something. "And then she's going straight to the airport."

"Airport?" I say. "Why is she going to the airport?"

Marguerite looks at me in surprise. "She didn't tell you?"

"Tell me what?"

"Hmm," she says. "That's interesting." She glides across the room toward another pile of dresses.

"What didn't she tell me?" I ask.

Half an hour later we're in the back of a town car on its way to JFK. Turns out Marguerite and Ramie are off to London together to shoot with this hot new photographer who's on the verge of "blowing up." This trip is key for both of them because the "London mags," according to Marguerite, are where it's at nowadays. If they can get in with a few photographers and fashion editors there, they'll be able to "blow up" too. All of which is just fine and dandy, but I'm not going to the airport to wish Ramie a bon voyage.

I'm going to stop her.

I don't tell Marguerite this. I sit quietly next to her while the town car barrels treacherously down the Brooklyn-Queens Expressway. Marguerite is content to purr about how great it is that someone with Ramie's "provincial" upbringing "gets it"— "getting it" meaning, apparently, moving to London as soon as possible to dive headfirst into the "epicenter of editorial fashion."

Marguerite grew up in London but made the "absurd mistake" of assuming New York was the place to make it in fashion.

When she laughs about her naïveté now, it's with the light-hearted condescension only the truly wise can afford. She's even more beautiful when she laughs. My antipathy to her grows.

"New York is dead," she says. "Ramie's wise to realize that now, before she invests too much time here."

I don't tell Marguerite that if she thinks she's dragging Ramie to London with her permanently, she's out of her mind. I also don't tell her the giant rhinestone snail on her lapel is stupid. There are a great many things I don't tell Marguerite, because I am cultivating the tactic of surprise. As far as Marguerite is concerned, I'm a quiet, supportive boyfriend who only wants a nice kiss goodbye before disappearing into irrelevance so that his girlfriend can "blow up" in London. I achieve this feat of subterfuge by nodding silently at Marguerite's graceful patter while subvocalizing the words *I am going to kill you one day, you red-haired Ramie thief.*

"You really do look a lot like your sister," she says. "Have you dated Ramie for long?"

She doesn't know? Ramie hasn't told her even that small detail about me?

"All my life," I tell her.

"Hmm," she says. Then she looks out the window as if I were no more substantial to her than those wispy clouds in the sky.

Antipathy crosses the line into hatred.

Fueled by anger but committed to a calm exterior, I enter the British Airways terminal at JFK dragging one of Marguerite's gigantic suitcases. Ramie waits inside, sitting on one suitcase with another at her side. When she sees Marguerite, she jumps up and waves. Seeing me, her face travels briefly through surprise, then fear, before settling finally on guilty resignation.

I help Marguerite drag her suitcases to the check-in line, which switches back on itself twice. Ramie approaches me cautiously.

"What are you *doing* here?" she says.

"I could ask you the same question."

"Yeah," she says. "I thought I'd have time to see you at Marguerite's, but I got held up at one of the showrooms."

I nod. Marguerite busies herself by getting the plane tickets out of her purse.

"So how are you?" Ramie says. She touches my arm sympathetically, as if I've been ill recently. Then, remembering something, she says, "Mal, how's Jill? Did she . . ."

I stare at her.

"What?" she says. "What happened?" Something dawns on her suddenly. "Oh no." Her hands clasp in prayer around her face while she envisions the lurid possibilities. Then she lowers her voice. "Did you show up while she was there? With Larson?"

I keep staring at her. I have no interest in recounting Jill's aborted sexual adventures of the previous night, though for the record, I think it's appalling that Ramie failed to respond to Jill's text or comment on her outfit. She *knew* how important this was, how much Jill had built up the losing of her virginity.

"What aren't you telling me?" she says.

Ramie's tone draws Marguerite's attention briefly. The three of us shuffle forward in the check-in line. I'm still calm on the exterior, but something is building inside of me.

"Ramie?" I say, ignoring her queries entirely. "How long were you planning to be in London?"

Ramie's big brown eyes lock onto mine. "I know," she says. "I know. But Jack, you have to understand—"

"How long?"

She swallows. "A week?"

The word cuts through me like a jagged blade.

"I didn't know you were here," she says. "You keep coming early." Marguerite glances up, then moves forward a few feet to give us some space.

Ramie keeps her voice low. "It's impossible to plan anything around your cycle anymore."

"But you would have?" I ask. We kick the suitcases forward. "If you knew I was coming, you would have turned down this job with Marguerite?"

She stares at me, then takes a deep breath.

"So you wouldn't have," I say.

She sighs, then shrugs vaguely. "I don't know."

I push Marguerite's suitcase right up against hers. "What do you mean you don't know?"

My raised voice garners the attention of Marguerite and everyone in our vicinity. "Come here." I grab Ramie's wrist and try to pull her from the line so we can speak in private.

She resists.

"I want to talk to you," I say.

Ramie twists her wrist free. "We can talk here. I can't leave Marguerite with all the bags."

Marguerite sneaks glances at us while pretending to study her ticket. I stare Ramie down, resisting the urge (but only just) to throw her over my shoulder and drag her out of the airport.

"You have to stop doing this," she says. "You have to stop trying to control me."

But I'm not trying to control her. I'm trying to hold on.

"This is important," she says.

This, not *me.*

"Can't you understand?" she says. "It's my career we're talking about."

Her *career*? Three months ago she was goofing off at the beach all day with me. Just yesterday she was a college freshman. When did she acquire a career?

"All I know," I say, "is that every time I show up, you disappear."

"And all *I* know," she says, "is that every time something important happens for me, you try to hold me back."

We stare at each other in silence for a few seconds, then push the suitcases around the bend. The people behind us, sensing danger, leave a larger than normal gap between themselves and us.

"Just come outside with me," I say.

"No."

A security guard, alerted to our disagreement, eyeballs us menacingly. I don't fancy my chances with him. It might be a federal offense to argue with your girlfriend in an airport.

Quickly I change tactics. Pressing up against Ramie gently, I bring my lips to her ear. "I need you," I whisper.

She shakes me off and tries to inch forward, stopped only by her suitcases.

I stay on her. "Come on," I say. "I'm your one and only, remember? There's no one else like me. No one in the world."

"Stop it," Ramie says, but softly, without conviction. And she doesn't shake me off. I know how her mind works. As irritated as she is with me for trying to hold her back, whatever *that* means, she's even more thrilled by my single-minded commitment to getting her home. The urgency of my hunger is her number one turn-on. This I know. And oh, how I've exploited it.

"Stop being coy," I tell her. "You know where you belong."

"What do you mean?" she says.

To the offense and discomfort of everyone around us, I pull her close and wrap my arms around her. "You belong with me," I say.

I can feel the collective cringe around us. Not only does it not bother me, it fuels me.

"Forget London," I say. "Let Marguerite assist herself."

Big mistake. The word "Marguerite," despite being delivered with a pointed sneer, awakens something in her.

"Stop it!" she says with a powerful shove.

The security guard, previously regarding us with reluctant curiosity, comes over now.

"I'm going to London," she says. "You have to deal."

"I'm not dealing," I say. The airspace between our bodies enrages me.

The security guard walks right up to us now. "Is there a problem?"

Ramie and I both look at him.

"Can I see your tickets?" he says.

Marguerite steps over the bags. "I've got them," she says.

While the guard flips through Marguerite's tickets, Ramie and I stare each other down. Without words, I broadcast my intense disappointment with her. How can she resist my seductive powers? I'm her love god. That's what she's always telling me. At least it's what she always *used* to tell me. But Ramie is silently broadcasting something else now. A pigheaded resolve.

While we stare at each other in stubborn silence, people around us shuffle nervously, intrigued by the unfolding drama but fearful of being injured by it.

"I only see two tickets here," the security guard says.

I ignore him. I ignore everyone but Ramie. The need to be alone with her overwhelms all other concerns. If we are not in the back of a taxi within *minutes,* I'll self-destruct. I'm sure of it.

The guard steps forward. "Which one of you is Ramie Boooly—Boolyoox?"

I'm only dimly aware of Marguerite trying to neutralize him. The rest of my attention is focused on Ramie.

"If you leave today," I tell her, "it's over."

Ramie's mouth drops open. "You're making me choose between you and my career?" she says.

"Yes," I say.

"But—"

"Choose."

In the background, the security guard uses words like "has to leave" and "no ticket." I should be concerned, but the only thing that matters to me is Ramie's face and the failure of the words "screw London" and "you're all I need" to tumble sighingly from her lips.

The next thing I know, the guard's hand is on my arm. I don't resist. My iron certainty has gone limp, given way to the inevitability of defeat. I let him peel me out of the check-in line, away from Ramie, who watches me go without moving. When the security guard has led me all the way to the door, I turn around and shout, "If you leave now, don't ever come back!"

Ramie's nose wrinkles as she stares at me. She's on the verge of tears. I *want* her tears. Even more than I want her to come with me now, I want her to suffer.

The security guard deposits me outside, then goes back in. Ramie turns her back to me and rests her head on Marguerite's shoulder. The gesture sends a bullet to the base of my spine. My knees buckle, and I almost drop to the cold, cigarette-strewn pavement.

Eventually the guard comes out and tells me to leave. I don't remember which words he uses, only the tinge of pity in them. His pity is irrelevant to me.

Later, I find myself on the subway. It's a long, confusing ride back to the apartment. I wind up in Manhattan at one point and have to retrace my journey. When I finally make it back home, only the one-armed mannequin awaits me. There is a hush in the stale air as we stare each other down.

"She's gone," I say. "She chose her career over me."

I don't go into the details. There's a film of dreamlike uncertainty over the whole thing. Eighteen-year-old college freshmen don't have *careers*. At times I can't believe it happened. I suspect that the ride with Marguerite was just a lucid dream, or something I invented. That Ramie's still in "the city," doing pickups or studying for a test. She'll be home tomorrow, and we can put this whole episode behind us.

I spend the next two days taking long walks in circles around the neighborhood while trying to make sense of Ramie's irrational behavior. I don't get very far, and eventually frustration and anger give way to old-fashioned loneliness. I even toy with the idea of apologizing, not because I'm wrong, but because I can't bear her absence.

I've known solitude before. Recall that I spent most of my life alone in Jill's bedroom. But solitude has freshly visceral characteristics now. Ramie's absence is physical, like a missing limb. Even silence is newly malignant, a tight-fitting helmet.

For better or worse, though, I'm constitutionally incapable of faking an apology just to win her back. Maybe it's stubbornness or an inability to lie. Whatever it is, if I were a Shakespeare character, it would be my tragic flaw.

Ironically, it would be Ramie's too.

The third afternoon, when I can no longer tolerate the silence, I decide to call Daria. She answers on the first ring.

"Jill!" she says. "Oh my God. I can't believe it's been so long. How *are* you?"

When I tell her it's me, the joy drains right out of her.

"Sorry," I say.

She takes a moment to manufacture fake delight at hearing from me. "No, no," she says. "It's *great* to hear from you. How's it going? Is Jill okay?"

"Yeah," I say. "How are things at UMass?"

"Oh mal," she says. "You would not be*lieve* what happened to me." She goes into this long, meandering story about these "raging sluts" who live in her dorm and live-cam their sexual exploits online. While I'm listening politely, I realize that Daria is no fountain of consolation. Nor is she even *my* friend. She remained supportive of Jill throughout the summer, but she never fully accepted me. Though too polite to openly reject me, she acted like I was a danger-ous puma Ramie had unwisely acquired as a pet. I constantly forgave her for this. It's what you do with Daria. But I get noth-ing from this conversation. I can't relate to her dorm story at all.

"So what's up with you and Ramie?" she asks finally.

In the end, I decide to spare her the details because it would only upset her. "Nothing much," I say. "Same old same old."

"Well, um, I kind of have to meet this friend?"

"That's cool," I say. "I'll tell Jill you said hi."

"Deeply!" she says. "And Ramie too. Tell them to call me!"

"I will!" I say with faux enthusiasm.

When I hang up, I realize the whole conversation ate up only five minutes. And I'm just as alone as before.

That night, while I'm waiting for the mean lady to hand me my slice of pizza to go, I commit the profoundly desperate act of texting Tommy Knutson the following:

S.O.S. Jck

He doesn't text back.

Oh, don't go spilling any tears for me. This has been a life of hard knocks. Believe me, I never thought it would be easy. I just have to toughen up is all. I'm Jack McTeague, remember? I survived the Evil Snow Queen of Winterhead. It's going to take more than the wrongheadedness of a temporarily insane girlfriend to plunge me into the mopey hole for good. I just need to buck up and be a man or whatever.

Oddly, it's when I stop to think about Jill that I'm able to envision a way out of the gloom. Jill would put a strict time limit on her marination in self-pity. After that she'd hatch some harebrained scheme like tarting herself up to go shag some skeletal hipster or changing her hairstyle. She'd *do* something. That's one thing I respect about Jill. She's a doer. A vilely manipulative one at times. But a doer, nonetheless.

So on day four, while trying to hatch a gloom-defeating scheme of my own, I find myself standing outside the dog run at the perimeter of McCarren Park. I like watching the dogs, the way they sniff each other and zigzag around. Every once in a while one dog climbs onto another dog and either gets bucked off or welcomed aboard. I respect the directness of that.

"You up for a bit?"

"Sure, why not."

This gives me an idea.

Yes, I know it's potentially unwise to get ideas from dogs. But look, it's not like I'm surrounded by a council of wise beings. The dogs are what I have.

I take out my cell phone and text:

I'm single now FYI.

You know who I send it to?

Natalie.

After I send it, I lean against the fence and wait to see if she calls back. Meanwhile, there's this little greyhound chasing the crap out of a much larger husky. When the husky stops to bark at it, the greyhound backs off for a second, then resumes the chase. They repeat this little game over and over again with no dilution of fervor.

Eventually my cell phone rings.

"Jill?" Natalie says.

"It's Jack," I say.

"Oh," she says. "Hi. Why do you guys share a cell phone? Is that a twins thing?"

"Yes," I say. "Did you get my text?"

"Uh-huh," she says.

"So?"

"So?" she says.

"Want to hang out or something?"

"Or something?" she says.

"Yeah," I say. "Come on, meet me somewhere. I'm bored. And single. Did I mention that I was single?"

I can hear the hesitation on the other end. I don't know Natalie well enough to say whether it's nervous excitement or true ambivalence, but all of a sudden I'm desperate for her to invite me aboard. *Oh please oh please oh please, invite me aboard,* I think.

"Menesale's," she says finally. "North Eleventh and Berry."

When we hang up, I stare at the dogs for a few more minutes. The greyhound is still chasing the husky, and the husky is still tolerating it. Or flirting. It's hard to tell. Maybe the husky just had its heart stomped by a careless girlfriend who loves her career more than him. Maybe that husky is hoping for a little affection from the greyhound to take its mind off its sorrows. It doesn't mean the husky doesn't love its girlfriend. It would take its girlfriend back in a heartbeat. But sometimes a dog needs a little TLC.

Menesale's is an empty Italian wine bar. I find a booth in the back and wave off the waiter because I know nothing about wine and am not even sure he'll serve me. I'm not here for the wine.

When Natalie enters, she speaks with the bartender, who nods eagerly. Then she comes over and joins me.

"Do you even drink wine?" she says. "I figured you didn't, so I ordered you a glass of Montepulciano. I know the bartender, so he won't card you. Just try not to look eighteen."

"Eighteen and a half," I say.

"You look awful," she says. "What happened?"

"Long story," I say. "Ramie sort of dumped me. What do you mean by awful?"

"What do you mean by sort of?"

I shrug in an effort to be nonchalant.

"You look tired," she says. "That's all."

"But still devastatingly handsome?"

Natalie doesn't answer, though she seems amused by me, which is a start at least.

The bartender comes over and deposits two glasses of red wine on our table. Suddenly, getting drunk seems like an excellent idea. If Natalie turns me down, I'm not sure what I'll do. I can't be alone anymore. Alone is off the table, a nonstarter. I'm through with alone. While Natalie swirls the wine gracefully in her glass, I take a big gulp.

"Should I get you a straw?" she says.

I swallow the mouthful. "No, I'm good."

Natalie clinks her glass against mine.

"To singlehood," she says.

"Right," I say.

We both drink.

"I have this book on wine," she says. "And Montepulciano is supposed to taste like cherry. Do you taste cherry?"

"No," I say.

"Me neither."

"I taste wine, though."

She puts her glass down and pulls a laptop from the bag at her side. She opens it and taps the space bar to wake it up. "So what's your plan? Mope around for a week, then hit the streets in search of new blood?"

"Is that what people do?" I say. "I've never been dumped before."

She stares at me for a second, then returns to her keyboard. "Read this." She turns her laptop toward me.

On the screen is the girl-trader article, "Sleeping with the Enemy." It's only a paragraph long.

"It's short," I tell her.

"Yeah, Ian's not very quotable," she says. "Anyway, I wanted to lead with the visuals." She reaches over and taps the keyboard, revealing a mock-up of the infamous chart, with labels describing its lurid components.

"It looks great," I tell her. "Very damning."

She pulls the laptop back. "I know. Next time you can do the interview."

"Cool."

"Throw yourself into work," she says. "That's the best way to get over someone."

"I can think of another way."

She laughs. "I'm sure you can." She starts typing again.

"What are you doing?" I say.

She holds up her finger to tell me to wait; then she finishes typing and turns the laptop toward me.

It's opened to the casual encounters section on craigslist. In a new listings window, she's typed:

Hot M4W 18 "sort of" dumped by gf seeks consolation/revenge sex

"Do you have a photo?" she says. "You get more traffic with a photo."

"Very funny."

She pulls the laptop back to her side of the table. "Cheer up," she says. "You picked the right city to be single in. You have math on your side. Six to one, I think."

"Six to one what?"

"Single straight girls to single straight guys. It's a total conspiracy."

"Yeah," I say. "But I don't need six girls."

"Uh-huh." She keeps typing. "Here's one for you." She reads from the screen. " 'Curvaceous w4m looking for fun in Brooklyn.' " She presses her lips together. "Curvaceous means fat. Do you like fat?"

I shrug.

What ensues is a tour of the slutty and desperate of craigslist with Natalie as my tour guide. She focuses mainly on Brooklynites in search of instant gratification, but to my surprise and hers, none of it appeals to me. I am, however, beginning to feel warm and light-headed from the wine, which *does* appeal to me.

"Okay, what about her?" Natalie says.

She shows me a snapshot of a blond girl licking a lollipop, with the caption "Candy 4 U. Candy 4 me."

It leaves me cold. "No thanks," I say.

"Man, you're picky. My guy friends are always complaining about how hard it is to get laid. Like girls have it easier or something. It's so not true. You just have to know where to look."

"Why are you doing this?"

"I'm trying to help," she says.

"But I don't want that kind of help."

"I know." She keeps typing. "You want me to be your back-board."

"My backboard?"

"For rebounding," she says. "But it's not in the cards. Sorry."

"Why not?" I say. "I know you're interested."

She stares at me coldly.

"Jill told me," I say.

"Bitch."

"It's cool," I say. "I like you too." I take a big sip of wine.

"Don't chug it," she says.

I take another big sip. "Let's get drunk together."

"Jack," she says. "I'm not having revenge sex with you."

"Why not?"

She narrows her eyes at me, so I lean back in the booth to let her have a good look. "We're both single. We both want it. What's the big deal?"

She has a small sip of wine. "It's not happening," she says.

"Oh, come on!"

This comes out louder than I had anticipated, which attracts the attention of the bartender. Natalie looks at him nervously, then leans over the table and whispers loudly, "Are you already drunk?"

"Possibly." I take the glass of wine and sink back into the booth with it. I take another throat-burning gulp.

Natalie rolls her eyes and looks at the door.

"Oh, what's this?" I say. "Are you *withholding* your *commodity*? Are you inflating its value? Go ahead. Leave if you want to. It'll drive me wild and make me want you even more."

"Why are you being like this?"

"Why are you being such a tease?" I can hear my own words slurring.

"What did you just call me?"

"A tease."

Natalie stares at me in shock for a few seconds; then she takes a large sip of wine. "Okeydokey," she says. She reaches into her bag, pulls out a twenty, and slaps it on the table. "I'm going now." She slides the laptop into her bag.

"Wait," I say. "That came out wrong."

"Did it?"

"Sort of," I say. "If I said it differently, would you come home with me?"

Natalie shakes her head in continued disbelief at what I'm saying. I'm drunk. I realize that. But I'm only being honest.

"Teach me," I say.

Natalie's eyes blink very rapidly.

"I'll do whatever you tell me," I say.

Natalie keeps staring, wide-eyed. I think I'm blowing her mind right now. But not in a good way. Not in a way that will convince her to come home with me.

"Look," I say. "I know I'm young, and I don't understand the ways of the world or anything. I don't, for example, understand about commodities and Saudi Arabia or whatever. But

• JACK •

I'm willing to learn. So long as sex is part of it. I really need to learn about that."

"Did Jill relate our *entire* conversation to you?"

"Yes."

"Why?"

"Who cares?" I say. "All I know is that I need to have sex with you or at least lie down with you and hold you and stuff. Is that wrong? It doesn't feel wrong. I mean I can say it differently if you want me to. How should I say it?"

She shakes her head. "I don't work like this."

"Do you want me to beg?"

"Please don't."

"I can plead," I say. "I'll do anything. I swear. There is nothing I won't do to have sex with you right now. Do you understand that? Nothing."

"No way," she says. "It's not happening."

Nevertheless, we end up at her place.

At the kitchen counter, she pours us another two, completely unnecessary, glasses of wine while I lift the hair off the back of her neck and kiss the soft skin there.

Natalie does not smell like Ramie. She smells like flowers, lovely spring flowers, which is fine. It is in no way necessary for a girl to smell like musk and coconut, which is what Ramie smells like.

When Natalie turns around to hand me a glass of wine, I lean in and kiss her very softly on the lips. Her lips are nothing like Ramie's, and my heart rebels.

I override it.

If Jill can do this sort of thing, so can I.

I pull back and look at Natalie. She's very pretty in her own way. Her eyes are pale and bright. She drinks her wine quickly.

I'm already drunk, so I put my glass down and guide Natalie over to her couch.

Once there, we kiss for a long time. I can feel Natalie's hesitation giving way to desire. She slides on top of me, letting her long, flower-smelling hair fall on either side of my face.

I close my eyes and let my arms encircle her. But her waist feels so strange. Her knees and hips and everything else fall in foreign configurations. I try to disappear into her, to let lust take over. That's how Jill got through it with Larson—before I showed up anyway. She stopped thinking and let her body take over.

I am a sex machine, I say to myself. If Jill can do it, so can I.

Natalie's lips caress my cheek.

Let go, I tell myself. Let Natalie take over. She's done this before. She knows what she's doing. It in no way matters that I'm in love with someone else.

I am a sex machine.

Natalie kisses my neck. As I look down at her, I notice the auburn roots of her hair. Something about it makes me turn away.

What's wrong with me? Natalie is beautiful. Beautiful enough anyway. The smooth sensual motion of her body is the medicine I need. Surely I deserve it after all I've been through. Surely I deserve one moment of comfort.

I run my fingers through her hair, but everything feels wrong.

"Stop," I hear myself say. "Please stop."

Natalie looks up at me, surprised and hurt. "What's wrong?"

I shake my head. "I can't," I say. "I . . . I . . ."

Natalie sits up, straddles my hips, and looks down at me. All I want is to run away. Even the sight of her is suddenly offensive. And that flower smell is all wrong. I start to pull myself out from underneath her, but she's up and off the couch in one quick move.

"Natalie?" I say.

She puts her hand up as she walks away, then grabs her wineglass and downs it in one go.

"It's not you," I say.

She doesn't say anything, but I see her shoulders rise suddenly in laughter. I want to say something comforting. I truly am grateful for the way she offered herself to me. I even sort of love her for it. But also, and bewilderingly, I can't stand being in her presence right now. It feels like a moral affront just standing there. I want to be home. I want to be anywhere but there.

"Sorry," I say.

She shakes her head and walks away to her room.

I grab my coat and let myself out.

●

(re)cycler

I will never do that again. I will never play with a girl's affections or use her for consolation. It's monstrous. Not so much for the sickening feeling it arouses in me, but for the cruel reflection of it in her eyes. Watching Natalie see my desire turn to disgust is a thing I will never forget. She didn't deserve that. I've never been more ashamed of myself.

november 22

●

Jill

The more you know a person, the stranger he seems.

It's the day before Thanksgiving, and I'm on a train heading for Boston with a head full of Jack and a broken heart.

The memories come so easily now. All I have to do is close my eyes. There I am running half naked down the street, with Ian in hot pursuit and Jack's thing flopping precariously between my thighs.

Flash forward.

Now I'm underneath Natalie, with her flower-smelling hair and Jack's lukewarm desire coursing through me.

Flash backward.

My breath fogs the window at JFK while I watch Ramie rest her head on Marguerite's shoulder.

I see it all. But I don't understand it any more than Jack did.

When a woman walking through the aisle bumps my foot with her suitcase, my eyes open and something drips down my cheek. I wipe my eyes. Across the aisle, a little girl stares at me, her hand stuck half into a bag of chips and her face contorted in empathic sadness. When I smile bravely, she turns away and burrows into her mother. Turning away myself, I lean my head against the window and watch the landscape blur by.

I'm accustomed to things in *my* life falling apart. But Jack's life was supposed to be stable. No matter what else was going on in our world, Jack loved Ramie and Ramie loved Jack. It was a law of the universe, unchangeable and undeniable. Like cosmic background radiation, it was always there. You could take it for granted. I know *I* did. I never realized how much until now.

On the drive from Boston to Winterhead, my parents grill me on what's happening in my life. I abridge. Heavily. I can't bear to talk about Jack and Ramie, and the other Big Story is the mortifying denouement of my "like, dinner" with Ian. I'm not going to set *that* scene for them. Instead, I tell them about work, which is comfortably boring, and about how much money I'm saving, which I exaggerate slightly.

Mom knows I'm omitting things, but being clairvoyant, she must also know that those *things* are of an uncomfortably sexual nature, so she doesn't push. Nor does she pester me about college, which I find surprisingly annoying. In the scheme of things, college seems like a manageable problem now. Instead, she asks me about Jack. And not with the usual distasteful tone either. Weirdly enough, it's as if she cares about *his* welfare and not just my own.

"I'm glad you stopped hating each other," I say.

Mom turns around and looks at me in surprise. "I never hated him, honey. I just . . ." She looks out the window for a second. "I just loved you." She reaches over and scruffs up my hair.

Behind the wheel, Dad laughs mysteriously. "Sometimes love makes you do crazy things, kiddo. *Crazy* things."

I can't disagree.

Everything at home is different now. Dad's moved back upstairs. The basement has been cleaned, sanitized, and deyogafied. All that remains of those days is Dad's yoga mat, which hangs now in their bedroom closet. Mom says he does it in the living room now, early in the morning while she's getting ready for work. Sometimes she does it with him, though she's "not sure about the chanting."

At first all this change is disorienting, but within hours it feels as if it's always been this way. As if we're all merely reverting back to the family life we should have been living all along.

Thanksgiving dinner with Auntie Billie and Uncle Steve proceeds without a hitch, everyone agreeing that my new look is *"très chic."* Auntie Billie, however, thinks I should "eat something once in a while" and wonders aloud if New York has run out of food. I find their attention soothing, their never-ending appraisal of how urban and cosmopolitan I look secretly thrilling. Mostly, I appreciate the predictability of it all. No matter what happens elsewhere in the world, Thanksgiving dinner will always be more or less like this.

After dinner, Uncle Steve, as he always does, palms me a twenty as if it were contraband. While the four of them retire for Baileys Irish Cream in the living room, I go upstairs to have a nap. But I don't sleep. I lie on my bed and listen to their spirited voices discussing nothing of any importance. Guiltily, I find myself wishing I never had to leave.

Somehow the McTeague family home, formerly a frostily coexisting collection of freaks, has transformed into a comforting, dare I say it, *normal* household. Maybe all I had to do was leave.

Over the next few days I avoid all of the impromptu gatherings of returning Winterhead High students, but I do touch base with Daria. She reports that the lead theory among my former classmates has changed from "Oh My God Jill McTeague Was a Transvestite All Along!" to "It Was a Prank, Authored by Ramie of Course." Ramie's absence from Winterhead over Thanksgiving break is attributed to her being in jail, pregnant, or in a psychiatric ward. I'm surprised by my own tepid reaction to this. But my former classmates, whose opinions mattered so much at one time, belong to my past.

The hardest thing for me is being in Winterhead without Ramie and Tommy. It makes me feel farther away from them than I've ever been.

Ramie's absence is not, however, the result of her being crazy, pregnant, or in jail. She's still in London, where's she's decided to stay for "a while." When she calls me Sunday morning, I'm eager to hash things out with her on the subject of Jack. I need to know just how broken their relationship is—if it's merely wounded or terminal. This is not just for Jack's sake, but for my own too. I can't bear the thought of them being apart.

Unfortunately, Ramie says she can only speak for a sec because it's a gazillion dollars a minute to call from there.

"Do you hate me?" she asks. "Does *he* hate me?"

"No and no," I tell her.

I insert a meaningful pause there, in the hope that she'll expand on the subject, but she doesn't. Instead, she sighs in relief, then tells me that London is "the dog's bollocks," which apparently is a good thing. Her parents are beside themselves with worry, of course. Like Jack, they don't understand how "crucial" it is that she work with the right people. Honestly, neither do I. To me it seems reckless to jeopardize her grades by skipping so much school, not to mention the terrible strain she's putting on her relationship with Jack.

But here's the difference: I have faith in Ramie. When she cares about something, she does all the research. She doesn't go off half-cocked. If she's willing to jeopardize so much to be in London, it's because London is important to her.

"I knew *you'd* get it," she says. "I just wish . . ."

Her voice trails off. I know she's thinking about Jack, and believe me, I want to jump right in and demand to know what she plans to do about him. But I know if I push, she'll only dig in her heels. That was Jack's big mistake.

"We can talk about him if you want," I say. "I'm deeply okay with it."

"Thanks," she says. "But . . ." Her voice trails off again.

At first I'm surprised she doesn't want to get into the

nitty-gritty with me. What are BFFs for if not endlessly co-analyzing the messy problems of infuriating relationships? But sometimes you have to work things out on your own. I know. I've been there. Besides, I'm not sure I can be objective about their relationship. In my mind, they belong together, and all other issues are secondary.

"It's okay," I tell her. "I'm here when you need me."

"Thanks," she says. Then she changes the subject. "So you don't think I'm nuts? You know, by staying in London?"

"No more than usual."

She laughs. The truth is, I don't actually "get" why she's risking so much to be in London. But I don't *expect* to understand everything Ramie does. If I did, she wouldn't be Ramie.

Forgetting that was Jack's other big mistake.

By the time I'm back on the train heading to New York, stuffed, rested, and twenty dollars richer, I feel as if my old life has slipped effortlessly away. This is precisely what I wanted, of course, but I can't help feeling a little sad about it. It wasn't *all* bad. There were some good times. There'll be good times again too. Won't there?

Those first few days back in New York, I find myself in a bit of a funk. Ramie's not around, and in her place is an e-mail alert from PayPal telling me she's deposited her half of the December rent into my account. I'd gladly exchange the money for some face time. Natalie's too busy with her magazine to spend any time with me, though she promises to buy me a margarita as soon as things calm down.

There are eight million people in New York City, but mal, is it hard to make friends. I mean, sure, they're pleasant enough on the surface. If you ask someone for directions, they're quick to offer assistance. Other than the mean lady at the pizza place, most of the store clerks and waiters are cordial and sometimes downright friendly. Even the bankers, insurers, and lawyers who temporarily employ me are pretty nice. But for all that, the city is a lonely place. Its bustling masses only reinforce that point.

The one person I can claim to know in any meaningful way in this city is Ian. But as you might recall, our last encounter did not exactly end on a high note, and I have no idea what to do about that.

I have taken to heart my dad's warning about how a series of small mistakes can add up to big disaster. I don't want Ian to be one of those mistakes. Nor do I want to wind up on that precipice, staring into a future I don't even want. I'd like to avoid the precipice altogether if possible.

Since I find myself day after day in a business-type environment, one afternoon I decide to approach the problem of Ian the way business people approach everything: with bullet points.

In business-speak, they call this "chunking." Thus the large, miasmic problem of how to deal with Ian breaks down into the following more manageable chunks:

- Ian might suspect I am sometimes Jack.
- Ian might find above less than alluring.
- Virginity, now a terminal disease, is beginning to glow.

Once I've centered this on the page and chosen the right font, I print it out and take it home with me. Every once in a while I unfold it to see if any solutions come to mind.

Then one day I'm working at this law firm where—and I'm not exaggerating here—*nothing* happens all day long. I swear, the phone rings once. That's it. This allows me to create the following PowerPoint presentation:

Possible Solutions to the Three-Chunk Ian Problem: A Lesson in Precipice Avoidance

SOLUTION #1: INVENT A NEW LIE, SUCH AS JACK
IS A DANGEROUS PSYCHOPATH WHO STEALS MY COATS.
Benefits
• Preserves real secret
• Makes me seem vaguely heroic
Liabilities
• Smears self with tarnish of familial psychopathy
• Impugns Jack

SOLUTION #2: DO NOTHING. WALK AWAY. WRITE IAN OFF.
Benefits
• No further action required
• Slight chance of Garbo-like mystique
Liabilities
• Need to recruit new devirginator
• Loneliness, oh the loneliness

As you can see, despite the orderliness of the presentation, both solutions pretty much blow. I spend a long time adjusting the formatting and changing the fonts, but it's no better in Helvetica. In Times New Roman it just looks pompous.

While I stare at it in this punishingly quiet law office where nothing *ever* happens, I can't help but notice the fact that Ian has made no attempt to contact *me* since that fateful night. I think—though one can never be sure—that if *I* were in Ian's shoes, I would have made *some* effort to verify that the girl I almost devirginated made it home safely after fleeing my apartment practically naked. But then Ian is probably wondering—if he's thinking of that night at all—how Jack wound up in *my* coat. Perhaps Ian thinks he was the victim of a mean-spirited prank. Perhaps he's wondering why *I* haven't called *him*. There could be whole chunks I haven't considered.

I reorganize all the data into a spreadsheet and print that out.

Then one day I'm on my lunch break at this diner in midtown, picking through soggy coleslaw with the spreadsheet at my side, when my cell phone rings. I realize it's hardly rung at all for days. I dig it out, hoping it's Ian, but it's not.

It's Tommy.

I stare at the letters TK, unable to move. To the annoyed stares and unsubtle harrumphs of other diners, I let it ring. The old man at the table next to me is so irritated he drops his spoon with a loud clang and glares at me.

I feel bad, but what does he expect me to do? Answer the phone and start talking? To Tommy Knutson? I'm completely unprepared. Answering the phone right now would be reckless.

I let the call go, then wait for the new voice mail icon to appear. While I'm waiting, the waitress comes by to ask if I'm finished, and I wave her off somewhat rudely. Agonizing seconds pass. The muddled hubbub of the diner seems to grow in volume as I stare at my cell phone, willing the new voice mail icon to appear. While I wait, my knee bounces manically under the table and I am unable to resist imagining possible left messages. Such as:

"Hi, Jill. I've been thinking. Life on the road is great and all, but I can't bear to live another day without you."

I hate myself for entertaining such childish thoughts. I was supposed to have put Tommy Knutson behind me. I cut the cord, remember? But while I wait for that icon to appear, I can't help but slip right back into the old longing, the old desire.

When the new voice mail icon appears, my heart beats so loudly I'm sure everyone in the diner can hear it. I take a deep breath, plunge into the wild and reckless hope that Tommy loves me after all, and retrieve his message.

"Hey, Jack. I got your text. Sorry I didn't get back to you sooner. My cell phone kind of died. I just put my SIM into a new one. I hope everything's okay. Call me and let me know, all right? I'm worried about you."

Click.

"What?!" I say out loud and to no one.

The old man at the next table, who really is too nosy for his own good, picks up his bowl of soup and moves to another table.

Hey, *Jack*? Tommy's worried about Jack? Why isn't he worried about *me*?

I try to calm down with some cleansing breaths, but this only intensifies my confusion.

Is Tommy's message coded? He put his *"SIM"* into *"a new one?"* Am I supposed to read something sexual into that?

I call the waitress over, get my check, and take the rest of my BLT to go.

As I stalk the crowded rush hour sidewalks of midtown, Tommy's message begins to enrage me. Then the fact that I'm so enraged by it enrages me further. When did the cord grow back? Will Tommy Knutson continue to break my heart for as long as I live? I don't want a permanently broken heart. I want to be over him.

I stop walking suddenly and look up at the bright blue sky.

That's when it comes to me in a brilliant flash of insight: the solution to all of my problems.

I've been thinking too small. In my effort to avoid making small mistakes, I've restricted myself to small solutions. But there are no small solutions anymore. Sometimes you have to think big.

I dig the cell phone out of my bag and type the following:

Sorry about the other nite. Much 2 xplain. Dexter's? Tonight at 7?

I send it to Ian, and less than a minute later he texts back:

Ok.

●

When I get home that night, I hash out the whole plan with the mannequin. I do the talking, but she smiles supportively. It's a simple plan. There are no carefully rehearsed deceptions or clever manipulations. I have no exit strategy or abort protocol.

What I do have is an outfit. My favorite black jeans, my red pouffy blouse, and Ramie's thick red corset belt. I put it on as if it were armor, but I doubt it will protect me from what I'm about to do. When I look in Ramie's full-length mirror, I can't help seeing Jack there. I dig around in Ramie's underwear drawer for her digital camera and pull up one of the less pornographic images of him. He does look just like me. I put on some dark eyeliner and pink blush, but I can still see him there beneath the surface. I guess it's appropriate, given that what I am about to do could arguably be described as Reckless and Stupid.

Before I leave the apartment, Mannequin assures me that everything will be okay. She has a good feeling about tonight. I'm owed a break, she says.

I want to believe this. But in my soul I know there is a distinct possibility of heartbreak.

There always is.

On my way down the stairs I hear music coming from Natalie's apartment. I stop outside her door for a second, then knock twice.

She opens it right away.

"Say something encouraging," I tell her. "I'm about to do something reckless and stupid."

"Okay." She pulls back and has a good look at me. "I like your belt?"

I'll take it. I nod and head down the stairs.

"Whatever you're doing," she says, "don't waste your one phone call on me. I have *no* money!"

Dexter's is crowded, and Ian sits at the bar, hunched over a can of Pabst Blue Ribbon. I walk right up to him and lean against the bar.

"So you're okay," he says.

I nod, then glance around in search of a free table. I point to one near a window in the corner next to a pile of coats. "You want to go over there?"

He nods and grabs his beer. Behind him, Joel the bartender waves shyly. It's pretty clear from Joel's face that he disapproves of my continued association with Ian, but Joel doesn't understand. Ian and I shared something that night. I'm not sure exactly *what,* but I'm not ready to walk away from him just yet, no matter how convenient it would be to do just that.

Ian and I lean against the windowsill and stare at the crowd gaily discussing whatever it is you discuss when you're not about to lay your whole soul bare.

"Um," he says. "I'm really sorry if I, like, did something that you didn't want me to."

"Oh," I say. "No. It's nothing like that."

" 'Cause I thought I was being gentle and stuff. I didn't think I was pushing you or anything."

"No, Ian, it wasn't that."

"Really?"

I nod. "Yeah. I liked what you were doing. I liked it a lot."

"You did?"

"Defo," I say. "Deeply. Yes."

"Oh." He lets out a sigh of relief.

So *that's* why Ian hasn't called. All this time he's been thinking I ran away from *him*. And here I was entertaining the possibility that he was a cold and callous person. But he's not. He's tender and kind. I never knew this because, despite our physical intimacy, I never knew *him*.

That's what it's like when you have a secret. You have to keep everyone at arm's length. They can't know you, so they can't love you. And you can't love them either. In some ways, they will always be strangers to you. And the people who do know your secret will always be precious.

"Ian," I say. "I need to tell you something really important."

"Okay," he says.

"I'm kind of a boy sometimes."

"What?" His face is blank, as if he hasn't heard me. "You're kind of what?"

Believe it or not, that was my plan. I told you it was simple.

"Did you just say you're a boy sometimes?"

"Yes," I say. "That's exactly what I said."

Ian stares blankly.

"Ian?" I say.

He keeps staring. It's like he's blacked out.

"Okay," I say. "You know Jack, my quote unquote brother?"

He nods very slightly.

"He's not really my brother."

Ian's mouth opens, but he says nothing. Very subtly, he inches away from me.

"We sort of share the same body," I say.

Ian's eyes dart around my face. "Are you telling me you're a transvestite?"

"No."

He takes a swig of beer, then looks at me in pained non-comprehension.

"How it works is . . . um . . ."

Ian's eyes drift down my body.

"It's all there," I say.

"What?"

"My girl parts."

Ian takes another large swig of beer.

"I'm a real girl," I say. "Just not all the time."

Ian shakes his head, but I can see realization dawning. The puzzle pieces click together. It's not a complete shock to him. He suspected the truth, but he must have dismissed it. Now that I'm confirming it for him, there's no escape.

This is the moment I was hoping for, the moment when Ian would become one of the precious few who know my secret.

"What *are* you?" he says.

It's not the question that hurts, it's the way he asks it. Less than a whisper, it slips out like a hiss, as if even to ask is to touch shame. A brand-new shame. An uncontemplated shame.

"I . . . I don't know what I am," I say. "But I know how I feel." I reach for his hand.

He pulls it away sharply.

"Ian," I say. "That night, before this happened, do you remember how you felt?"

Ian's breathing intensifies. He's remembering now. I can see it on his face. He's thinking of the way he touched me before he knew.

"It doesn't have to change," I say. "We can still . . ."

His eyes flick to the exit. "Why are you doing this?" he says. "Why are you telling me this?"

"I thought you'd want to know the truth," I say.

His head shakes in tiny little moves, just like my mother's when she doesn't want to accept something.

"Maybe it's too much to absorb right now," I tell him. "Do you want to take some time to think about it?"

"Okay," he says too quickly.

"Why don't I call you later," I say.

He nods aggressively, his eyes flicking to the exit.

"Like tomorrow?" I say.

"Okay." He stands up.

I put my coat on as slowly as possible to give him time to stop me from leaving.

"So I'll call you?" I say.

He nods, but he doesn't move. When I finally get my coat on, he reels back, as if terrified that I might kiss him goodbye.

I don't.

That walk to the exit through the dense, chattering crowd is the loneliest walk of my life.

Once outside, I peer through the steamy window and see him walking back to the bar. Someone waves to him and he waves back. When Joel notices Ian at the bar, he looks around for me.

I want to wave at Joel, to let him know I'm okay. But instead, I pull my coat tightly against the cold and run all the way home.

"Whoa," is what Ramie says when I call her that night to relay the whole conversation.

She has to whisper because she's crashing on someone's floor in London and doesn't want to wake her four other flatmates.

"Did I do the right thing?" I ask her.

She takes a second to think about it, but eventually says, "Yes. Defo. And it's his problem if he can't handle it."

"You don't think he can handle it?"

When she doesn't answer right away, I realize I may have made a grave error.

"No one's ever going to be able to handle it," I say. "Are they?"

"Don't say that," she says. "*I* can handle it. Daria can handle it. Tommy can handle it."

But that's a pretty short list. Will it always be so?

"Give him some time," Ramie says. "You never know. People can surprise you."

•

But when I call Ian the next day, he doesn't answer.

Two days later he still hasn't returned my call.

I guess Ramie's right. People can surprise you.

Late one night, nineteen days into my phase, as I'm lying in bed, I feel a faint rumbling from within. It could be all the popcorn and ginger ale I had for dinner, but there's a chance it's Jack waking up. I wish I could talk to him. It's strange, isn't it, that the only person in the world who could understand what I'm going through is a person I'll never meet.

Undoubtedly, Jack will find it laughably naïve that I ever thought Ian could handle our secret. In retrospect, it seems absurd to me. I guess that was the Stupid part of the Reckless and Stupid combo. But the funny thing is, I have no regrets. That moment was the first time in my life that I ever felt better than my circumstances. Not in control of them—that's a mad delusion—but not controlled by them either. No matter what life throws at me (and believe me, it throws some nasty stuff), I know I can handle it with dignity. My circumstances might determine what I am, but they don't determine who I am.

What I take from the whole episode (and Jack, I hope you remember this because you need to learn it too) is that you can't control how other people behave. No matter how much you need them, they are driven by forces beyond your control. All you can do is be brave.

But as soon as I think this, I sit up in bed and turn on the poodle lamp.

Have I been brave?

I mean *truly* brave?

Sure, I revealed my darkest secret, but only to a guy I'm not in love with. When you think about it, all I risked losing was a guy I'm not in love with.

How brave is that?

I get out of bed and find my cell phone on the dresser. If I'm going to be brave, I should be brave where it counts.

I turn on the phone, then sit on the edge of my bed with it. Within my short list of phone numbers is the even smaller sub-set of people who can handle my secret. I've been lying to one of them for far too long.

That's not brave.

I find the letters TK and press the call button. My heart beats faster with every ring. *I can do this,* I tell myself. *I just have to be brave.*

But after four rings, Tommy's voice mail picks up. "Hi, it's Tommy. Leave a message."

When I hear the beep, my breath leaves me. For a moment I fear that I am not up to the task. But when my breath returns, I summon my voice and say loud and clear what, in the past, I could only whisper.

"I love you."

It's been on the tip of my tongue for a long time.

I hang up, kill the poodle lamp, and lie down. Whether or not Tommy returns my call is something I can't cope with tonight. It's been a hard few days. In fact, it's been a hard few months.

But in those dizzy few seconds before slipping into oblivion, I feel certain that I've done the right thing, no matter the consequences. I have avoided the precipice. I'm sure of it.

That night, and that night alone, I sleep the dreamless sleep of the brave.

DECEMBER 13

●

Jack

All right, I have a confession to make.

In my attempts to distinguish myself from Jill, I may have judged her unfairly. I've called her naïve, deluded, manipulative, and all kinds of nasty things, and taken great pleasure in doing so. It's not that I was wrong. She can be all of those things. But it's only part of the story. If I'm completely honest with myself, I have to admit I've always sort of admired her. Never more so than now.

It's easy to forget that Jill has borne the brunt of our condition by virtue of the fact that she's the one who's been out there in the world posing as "normal." After all that's happened, I think it's safe to say that she's anything but. In fact, in some surprising ways she's extraordinary.

And if Ian Larson can't appreciate that, then screw him.

"Right, Mannequin?"

Mannequin just smiles, but I'm sure she agrees. She knows a jerk when she sees one.

I've been sitting on Ramie's floor all morning, leaning

against the doorjamb while scrolling backward and forward through Jilltime. I have a lot to think about, and Mannequin has been both wise and supportive. She's such an unlikely optimist too. I love that about her.

"But, Jack," she says. "Are you just going to sit there all day? Aren't you going to get up and *do* something?"

"Eh," I say. "I'd rather sit here and wait for Tommy Knutson to call."

I'm a little concerned he hasn't already. It took a lot of guts for Jill to leave that message. He better not fail her.

"Maybe his cell phone is broken again," Mannequin says.

I hope that's the case. I couldn't bear it if he rejected Jill right now. I'd have to head westward to kill him.

"Anyway," Mannequin says, "I hope you're not using Tommy Knutson as a distraction."

"From what?"

"Don't play dumb," she says. "From Ramie, of course."

"Well, jeeze, Mannequin, don't psychoanalyze me."

"Don't make it so easy, then."

I guess we've moved on to the tough love phase of our relationship.

"All right, all right," I say. "I've been a dick. I know. That ultimatum was a big mistake. I should have had faith. I should have embraced the beautiful mystery of Ramie's intangible motives."

"Well put."

"Thank you," I say.

Jilltime is a treasure trove of useful insights re: *moi* being

245

stupid about Ramie. And I do appreciate the way she dropped them in there for me to find. She's a smart girl. Possibly smarter than I am, and I touch genius from time to time. I'm beginning to see that if Jill and I were to combine the best of each other's traits, we'd be pretty amazing. Amazing and Wonderful, actually. We'd be almost superhuman.

There's something to aim for.

"Jack," Mannequin says. "You're stalling."

She's right. The funny thing is, I'm not even sure why. I know I have to call Ramie eventually, but I can't bring myself to do it yet. There's a certain peacefulness in sitting on the floor, not knowing what to do or how to do it. It's as if the mean, hungry world outside has ceased to exist and there's just me, Mannequin, and Ramie's fading scent. That's enough for now.

While I'm leaning against the doorjamb, slowly rolling my head back and forth to stretch out my cramping neck, I see something white slide across the living-room floor with a quiet *whish*. It's the first moving thing I've seen since I woke up. I stand up and grab it.

It's a small flyer advertising a launch party for Natalie's magazine, *Life Before the Apocalypse*.

I can just hear Natalie's footsteps out in the hall, quietly descending the stairs, followed by the careful opening and closing of her door. According to the flyer, the party is tonight.

For a moment I conjure a fanciful image of myself laughing and sipping a cocktail with Natalie and her magazine friends. I picture flowing fountains of champagne and elegantly dressed people making sharp, witty comments about stuff.

Then I realize Natalie probably intended this invitation for Jill, not me. After our last meeting, I doubt Natalie ever wants to see *my* face again.

"Hey, Mannequin?" I call out.

"What?"

I sit down on the couch and look at Natalie's flyer. "Would it be wrong to show up at Natalie's party?"

"Tough call," she says. "It's not like she wrote Jill's name on the flyer, right?"

It's true. But I'm not sure I can face Natalie after what's happened between us. I'm still ashamed of what I did.

"Hey, Jack?" Mannequin says. "Why don't you warm up for your apology to Ramie by apologizing to Natalie first?"

"Huh?"

"Think about it," she says.

I lean back on the couch to consider Mannequin's proposal. It seems ridiculous at first. But then I recall that this is precisely what Jill did. She got brave and confessional with Larson, then rode the confidence boost from that all the way to a love confession to Tommy Knutson.

"Wow, Mannequin. You and Jill are *geniuses.*"

"Duh," she says.

I get up, get dressed, head downstairs, and knock on Natalie's door before I have time to chicken out.

While I'm trying to calm myself down with deep breaths, I hear Natalie creep up to the door and turn the metal cover of the peephole. There is a long pause, where she is obviously, after seeing my face, weighing the possibility of pretending she's not home. But after a few seconds she turns the locks and opens the door.

She doesn't say anything, and neither do I at first. Suddenly, *I'm sorry* seems inadequate.

After a few awkward seconds I drop to my knees and take her hand in mine. "Forgive me," I say. "I was a jerk."

She says nothing, but she doesn't pull her hand away.

"It wasn't you," I say. "You were so beautiful, and I really did want you that day. It was just all this Ramie stuff. It's messing me up. I know that's no excuse. I shouldn't have walked out on you like that. And I shouldn't have left it this long without apologizing, but—"

"Did you join a twelve-step program?" Natalie says. She extracts her hand from mine and wipes it on her jeans.

I look up at her. "What do you mean?"

She stares at me with that confused look she gets when I've said something very ignorant. She does this with Jill too.

"Can you ever forgive me?" I ask.

"Were you raised in a secluded religious compound?"

I stand up. "Not quite. Natalie, I know what I did was wrong and cruel and—"

"Whoa, calm down. Jeeze. Are we talking about the same thing here? Are you referring to our very brief almost hookup?"

I nod.

"That's it?" she says. "That's what you're apologizing for?"

"Well, yeah," I say.

"But that was, like, *nothing.*"

"What are you talking about?" I ask. "It was monstrous. I seduced you and tried to play basketball off of you. And then—"

"Okay. Okay. I get it. I was there."

"Well, I'm sorry," I say. "You were generous and kind to me, and I'm really sorry."

She cocks her head to the side as she examines me. "You're so cute."

"No I'm not," I say. "I'm a user of girls. I'm . . ." I drop my head. "I don't even know what I am anymore. I talk to a mannequin."

"I see."

I look up. "Natalie, she talks back."

"Yeah," she says. "They usually do."

"What?"

"Did you get my flyer?" she asks. "Are you coming to the party? I need a lot of people to come. Young people. To prove how hip and unsafe the magazine is."

"You really want me there?"

"Of course," she says. "You're a contributor. You have to come. But—" She steps back a little and looks me up and down. "Do you own any other clothes besides jeans and T-shirts?"

I look down at my shirt. "Why?" I say. "Is there a dress code?"

"The dress code is no chumps. Why don't you go buy yourself an outfit or something? God, you and your sister. It's like you both want to blend into the scenery or something. Is that a twins thing?"

"I don't know."

"Are we good now?" she says. "Because I've got a million things today. Promise you'll come to the party."

"So you forgive me, then?"

"Jack," she says with an exasperated sigh. "I wasn't even mad at you. I really have to go. Come to the party."

She closes the door and I hear her thumping off into her apartment.

Forgiveness shouldn't be that easy.

When I return upstairs to ask Mannequin if it's true that I dress like a chump, she can't say. She spends most of her life naked. I suppose it is somewhat limiting to wear *only* jeans and T-shirts. It's not a trait you'd expect to find in the boyfriend of a brilliant up-and-coming fashion designer. Maybe if I took more of an interest in clothes, I wouldn't have accidentally insulted Ramie's profession. I make a mental note of this. When I do finally apologize for the ultimatum, it will make for a nice bonus apology. I think Ramie will admire that a lot.

In the meantime, I have to figure out what to wear to Natalie's party. Yes, I've decided to go. And no, it's not because I'm stalling on my apology to Ramie. I'm just waiting for the confidence boost to arrive.

I know nothing about men's clothes. Even when I mine everything Jill knows, I come up empty. On the subject of

men's clothes all she and Ramie have are a few opinions about pleats, which I consider an unacceptable gap for two people who profess to be fashion conscious. Men are half the world.

Since my closet has nothing but a few exact copies of what I'm already wearing, I decide to take Natalie's advice and get myself an outfit.

I head to Beacon's Closet, which was the sight of Jill's transformation from a bland girl who was "hostile to color" into the brightly colored babe she has become. I mean, uber-sophisticated vamp or whatever.

The place smells like old sneakers to me, and all the racks are jammed so close together you have to squeeze between them. Everything's organized by color, and I spend about ten minutes leafing through the dark blue rack before I realize they're all girls' shirts.

Glancing around, I spot a scrawny little guy with an ironic pompadour heading into another section. He seems to know what he's doing, so I follow him around and pick up shirts similar to the ones he picks up, but slightly larger. They're all variations on plaid. Once I've amassed seven, I take them to the dressing-room area in the back, where this short girl with oversize glasses folds clothes on a table. She looks up, leafs through my pile, and hands me a plastic number 7.

"Last one on the right's free," she says.

She has a cute smile.

Once in the dressing room, I decide very quickly that I do

not like plaid. I'm not a lumberjack. And what's with all the cowboy lines around the pockets? I return all seven shirts to the girl with the big glasses and go back to the men's section for some more.

When I take the new batch to her, she leafs through them again and says, "Yeah, I think these are better. Good luck!"

"Thanks."

I think she's flirting with me.

Most of the shirts are awful—itchy, too tight, and ugly to boot. But eventually I try on this shiny silver number that looks sort of old-fashioned and gangsterish. When I go out to look at myself in the big mirror, the girl looks up from her folding chores and nods approvingly.

"Sweet," she says. "Hey, hold on." She turns her back to me and digs through a pile of clothes on her folding table, then comes toward me with a white scarf.

"What's that?" I ask.

"Trust me," she says. "I know it's kind of strange, but . . ." She steps right up to me and ties the thing around my neck.

"Are you a fashion student or something?" For a second I fear this girl might know Ramie.

But she shakes her head. "Art history," she says. "I just like to play."

Ramie liked to play too, but only with Jill. When it came to fashion, she took no interest in me at all. Maybe that's why I always tuned her out when she talked about it. I knew it had nothing to do with me.

The girl sticks the ends of the scarf into the collar of the shirt. "I saw this English guy wearing one of these," she says. "And I swear it was the hottest thing ever. There." She steps back, then turns me toward the big mirror.

"What is this thing?"

"It's an ascot," she says. "It's very Thomas Jefferson."

"Is that good?"

She nods deeply. "He was the hottest founding father of all!"

I look at myself in the mirror again. It does look sort of elegant and old-fashioned.

"Could I wear this to a launch party for a magazine?"

"Yeah, wear it with those jeans. You look great."

"Are you flirting with me?"

"Not really." She goes back to folding clothes. "Just playing."

I turn away and look at myself in the mirror. I twist and turn a few times, but I find it hard to form an independent opinion on what I see. I know I'm irresistibly handsome, because that's what Ramie's always told me. But I can't be sure if the outfit is enhancing or detracting. I've never seen a real-life person wearing an ascot. I can only half recall a memory of Jill seeing one on a guy in a movie once. There's something unreal about it. In fact, the more I look at myself, the more unreal the whole image seems. I don't think it's just the ascot or this shiny silver shirt. It's all of me. It's like I'm seeing myself for the very first time.

"Are you okay?"

I turn to look at the girl folding clothes, and I must have a terrible expression on my face, because she looks worried.

"What's wrong?" she says.

I turn back to the mirror, but the person staring back isn't me anymore. He's a blank, an impostor.

"Are you going to be sick?" she says.

"I don't know," I say.

I return to the dressing room and close the curtain.

"Well, don't get sick in *there*," she says.

"Okay." I sit down and look in the mirror right next to me. I recognize all the pieces, but somehow they don't add up.

Do you want to know something? I'm *not* irresistibly handsome. I'm average. My eyes are smallish, and I have a boring nose. I'm not very tall, and my body is mediocre at best.

What made me think I was so good-looking?

I whip the curtain open and walk up to the girl at the folding table. "Can I ask you something?"

She nods but keeps folding.

"Tell me the truth," I say. "Am I average-looking?"

She stops folding. "That's a funny thing to ask a total stranger."

"Yeah, it probably is," I say. "But I need to know."

"You look a little pale," she says. "Do you want to sit down?" She moves a pile of clothes from an old wooden chair and tells me to sit.

"Thanks," I tell her. I can't see the mirror from there, which is a great comfort.

(re)cycler

The girl goes back to folding her clothes. "I don't think there's any such thing as average," she says. "Am I average?"

"No way," I tell her.

In truth, there's nothing exceptional or beautiful about her. She's a bit stumpy. And her gigantic glasses keep sliding down her nose. But she's so friendly, so kind, that to me she seems like an angel. And angels *are* beautiful.

"Is it okay if I just sit here?" I ask. "I can't face the mirror right now."

She nods. "I've had days like that."

I lean back in the chair and watch the other customers slowly browsing through the racks. The quiet screech of metal hangers and the whish of fabric on the folding table soothe me. After a while, though, I begin to feel as if I'm invading her space.

"So you think I should buy this scarf thingy?" I ask.

"It's an ascot," she says. "And yes. That and the shirt, and you should wear them both out of here. You'll feel better."

"I will?"

She nods. "Hold on." She digs a pair of scissors out of the pile of clothes on her table, then cuts the tags free and hands them to me. "Very few guys can pull off an ascot," she says.

"Are you sure I'm one of them?"

She nods. "There's something unique about you." She hands me the tags. "Just take these to the register."

"Okay."

While I'm paying, I realize she never told me if I was average-looking. And I no longer trust my own opinion.

●

It's cold and bright outside. The silver shirt feels strange against my skin and the silky ascot thing is surprisingly warm. But every time I catch a glimpse of myself in a storefront window, I shudder. The windows are not telling lies, though. It's not in their nature to lie.

I stop and stare into one. It's an old hardware store with an artless display of paint cans and dust mops. And right in the center is my face. It's not the face itself that bothers me. It's an okay face, I guess. It's the fact that I'm only now seeing it for what it is. It makes me realize I've been seeing myself through Ramie's eyes for most of my life. I was handsome because she thought I was. I was sexy because she had sex with me.

Even now, as I examine the white ascot bulging from the collar of this silver shirt, I can't help wondering what Ramie would think. I picture her appraising and critiquing it, but I can't appraise or critique it myself.

Is this what I've become?

I spent all that time trying to escape my Winterhead prison to have a real life of my own. And what did I do? I made myself a reflection of Ramie Boulieaux. That one skinny girl has borne the burden of my whole existence.

But that's no way to be. Even Jill, who's worshipped Ramie for most of her life, is at heart her own person. In fact, now that Ramie's not here to guide her every move, she's blossomed.

So why have I shriveled?

As I stare at my face in the dingy hardware store window,

my father's words come to me suddenly, courtesy of a crisp Jill-time memory: "I hated what I'd become."

Dad found himself standing on that precipice because of a series of small mistakes. Jill managed to avoid that fate by finding the courage to be honest, first with Larson, then with Tommy. But me? I must have made *thousands* of small mistakes somewhere along the line, because I am facing down the same horrible conclusion as my father. I hate what I've become.

I hate that I don't recognize my own face. I hate that I've been walking around with a bloated ego because Ramie thought I was sexy. I hate that I bought this ascot, not because I liked it, but because that girl at Beacon's Closet was nice to me.

I want to be better than this. I was going to be somebody, wasn't I? Not just some heartbroken, sex-starved (possibly ex-) boyfriend of somebody else. But somebody in my own right.

I pull myself away from the window with its dingy reflection of my mediocre face, then run back home. The necessity of my next decision becomes clearer with every step. There'll be no precipice avoidance for Jack McTeague. It's far too late for that. What I have to do now is drastic and terrible.

When I get to my building, I take a moment outside to catch my breath and stiffen my resolve. It's not confidence I need to do what I'm about to do. It's something bigger, something deeper. Moral fortitude, that's it. I need to know that what I'm about to do is the *right* thing.

Which it is. Trust me.

I run up the stairs and knock on Natalie's door. When she opens it, she screws up her face at me. "Are you wearing a cravat?" she asks.

"It's an ascot," I tell her. "I need you to do me a favor."

She looks suspicious.

I hand her my cell phone. "Keep this. Do not give it back to me, no matter what I say."

"Why?"

"There's a phone call I want to make, and I must be prevented from making it."

"You can just use a pay phone, though."

I drop my head in my hands. "Please, Natalie?"

"Okay," she says. "Fine. How long am I supposed to keep it?"

"Give it to Jill," I say. "She'll be back in a few days."

She nods. "Do you realize how strange you and your sister are?"

"Yes I do," I tell her.

I head upstairs to my apartment.

I am letting Ramie go. For real. Don't argue with me. It's the right thing to do. I can't go on feeding off of her for the rest of my life. It would only drive her away. It probably *is* what drove her away.

Besides, I'm Jack McTeague. I escaped a high-security prison. I helped make the world safe from girl-traders. I am not the kind of guy who needs a girlfriend just to be real.

I *am* real.

"Right, Mannequin?"

"Hell yeah!"

"You're my witness," I tell her. "Today I begin a new chapter."

"What's it called? You need a name."

"You pick a name," I tell her. "I have to get ready."

I won't lie. I spend nearly an hour crying in the shower. My commitment to letting Ramie go is like a punch in the gut, the righteousness of it ennobling, but not dimming the pain. Afterward, I get dressed in my new threads and try to get used to the way I look in the mirror.

From the other room Mannequin calls out, "Don't get so hung up on your appearance, Jack. Look at me. I'm missing an arm."

"Thanks, Mannequin," I call out. "And don't let anyone tell you that's a handicap either."

"I love you."

I fix my ascot as best I can and get the heck out of there before things get even weirder between me and Mannequin.

As you can guess, I'm feeling a little raw.

The party is in an art gallery near the L train. It's a small space. In the center is a towering robot sculpture made of Legos and plastic shopping bags. On the walls, Natalie has stapled blowups of the magazine pages. The place is packed with your usual Williamsburg denizens: ironic, scruffy, terminally cool. I remove my coat and dump it in the corner with the others. I am, of course, the only person in the room wearing an ascot.

But that's okay, I tell myself. I'm Jack McTeague and I wear what I want.

I do a slow perimeter of the room, eavesdropping on conversations and meeting people's glances with glances of my own. After a while, the gut-punch agony of Ramie's absence feels less like a weight and more like a hunger. But for what I can't be certain.

Eventually I spot Natalie near the bar, surrounded by guys. She looks beautiful in a tight black dress. When she spots me, she nods and gives me a quick, appraising up and down.

Not far away, a blowup of the infamous chart is pinned to the wall, and next to it is a crush of pretty girls. I prepare to go over and grandly take credit for it, receive their thanks, and tell them that as long as I'm here, they should consider themselves protected against the nefarious forces of Permascrew and his idiot posse.

But then I notice Perm and his idiot posse, dressed flamboyantly and standing in the midst of all the girls, smiling and laughing and having a grand old time. When Alvarez sees me, he breaks into a great big grin.

"Mayberry!" he says. I glance over my shoulder to see if he's talking to someone else.

"No, you!" he says. "Jack!" He waves me over. I walk over tentatively, and he takes my hand and whips it around in one of those funky jive handshakes. "You are one tricky S of a B," he says. He gestures toward the chart.

"What are you doing here?" I say.

"Yo, check it," he says. He points to some photos next to the chart, which feature him plus Perm and Sasha prancing around outside some derelict warehouses dressed as pimps! Sasha is wearing the vinyl jeans, and let me be clear on something, he looks even more ass-ish than you're thinking right now. No, seriously, turn it up a notch. Then another.

The three of them seem to have taken the satirical photo shoot as a fashion lesson because they're all dressed in imitation of their photos.

"Yo, Perm!" Alvarez says. He points his thumb in my direction. "Man of the hour."

Even Perm smiles at me. "Hey, man," he says. "I owe you one."

"What?" I lean in to Alvarez. "Why does he owe me one?"

"Dude," he says. "We're like celebrities now. Check this out." He taps Sasha on the shoulder.

Sasha turns around and faces us. He's holding a notebook and pen, and Alvarez takes it from him and shows me. Written inside is a list of girls' names.

"New blood," Alvarez says.

I glance at the cluster of pretty girls hovering around the chart on the wall.

Alvarez sidles up close to me. "They want to know what they can do to get on the chart." He raises his eyebrows suggestively. "We're trying to convince Natalie to make this a regular feature."

"But—"

• JACK •

"Seriously," Alvarez says. "You've got my marker. You ever in a jam, you need an emergency chick extraction, you pick up the phone. You got my digits?"

He stuffs his hand in his tight front pocket to pry out his cell phone, but just then Natalie approaches. She grabs me by the elbow, drags me to the bar, and hands me a plastic cup full of wine.

"Don't think," she says. "Drink." She grabs a bottle and re-fills her own cup. "So you went with the cravat?"

"It's an ascot."

"Uh-huh."

My eyes keep wandering back to Perm and company.

"Tell me about it," she says. "They've spun their humiliation into a harem."

"I don't understand," I say. "Why are girls *volunteering* to be on their chart?"

"Why do starlets get out of limos with no underwear?" she says. "There's no such thing as bad fame, I guess. Don't worry. I'm not making it a regular feature. I am, however, doing a story on those girls over there. You know, the new trend in self-objectification?" She clinks her plastic cup with mine. "Hey, maybe you should write it." She takes a sip.

I'm too stunned to follow suit. I can't *believe* Perm and his posse have turned this around. Where's the justice in that?

"Jack," she says. "It's a party. Come on, you're sucking all the joy out of the room."

"Sorry."

"Hey," she says. "See that unbelievably boring guy over there?"

She points to a middle-aged balding guy standing in front of a photograph of a girl in a snowsuit.

"Isn't that Kevin Jelivek?" I say.

She scrunches up her face. "How do *you* know Kevin Jelivek?"

I panic. "Um. Jill told me about him."

"You recognize him from Jill's *description*? Wow, is that a freaky twins thing too?"

I nod. "So, are you back together with him or something?"

"I don't know." She bites on her fingernail. "Do you think a guy who wears a gray suit every day can have a soul? You know what? Don't answer that. I have to go mingle. Please drink that." She backs away, but her eyes linger on my neck. "I take it back. I like your cravat."

"It's an ascot," I say again.

"Uh-huh," she says. "Why don't you go flirt with someone." She winks, then wanders off to mingle.

Kevin Jelivek watches her from a safe distance. I don't have any idea whether a guy in a gray suit can have a soul. My instincts, based on memories of Jill temping, say no. But I know what devotion looks like, and that guy is full of it.

I take a big sip of wine and glance around the party. Then I put in some time "mingling," but the sudden affections of Perm and gang make me want to hit something. The only girls who'll talk to me either want to hear about my involvement in "that chart thing" or provide useful criticism of my ascot.

• JACK •

I'm about to call it a night when I notice Larson in the corner, staring at me cagily. When I look at him, he looks away and stares at his old girl-trader buddies. Poor guy. He gave up all of *that* to impress Jill. And where did it get him?

I almost feel bad for him until I remember what he did to Jill. Then I want to punch him, which is a much more immediate and satisfying emotion.

When I walk over to him, he cringes but doesn't try to escape.

"Hello, dickhead," I say.

"What do you want?"

I lean against the wall right next to him. "I'm willing to entertain your apology," I say. "On Jill's behalf."

"Shut up."

"Ooh, good one," I say. "Hey, Larson, you want to know why she *really* fled your apartment that night?"

He narrows his eyes at me.

"Because of the way you smell." I take in a deep breath through my nose. "You really should do something about that."

He looks at the floor.

"Oh, come on," I say. "Don't be such a pussy." I push him in the chest.

"Stop that."

"Or what?" I say.

He looks straight at me. I stand a little taller to give him a bigger target. I *want* him to hit me.

"It's true," he says. "Isn't it?"

"What?" I say.

"You really *are* her," he says. "I didn't believe her at first. But . . . it's so obvious now."

"Oh yeah?" I say. "And what do you want to do about it?"

He keeps looking at me. I push him in the chest again, and he swats my hand away.

"I'm sorry," he says.

"Shut up."

"No," he says. "You're right. I *was* a dickhead."

"Agreed."

"I couldn't make sense of what she was telling me," he says. "But I've been thinking about it a lot and . . ."

"Wait a minute," I say. "Dude, I didn't come over here to listen to your *feelings*."

"Well, why did you come over?"

"To beat the living crap out of you," I say. "Duh."

"That's really mature."

"Oh, come on!" I say. "You turned your back on Jill when she was really vulnerable."

"I know," he says.

"No you don't. You don't have any idea what it's like."

"I know," he says.

"Stop saying I know!"

"I'm trying to apologize."

"I don't want your apology."

"But you just said—"

"I don't care what I said. Stop apologizing. What are you, a saint all of a sudden?"

"I feel really bad," he says. "Do you think she'll forgive me?"

"No!"

"Why not?"

My hands ball into fists. "You really are an ass," I say. "You know that?"

"I don't know why you hate me so much," he says. "*She* doesn't hate me."

I back away from him.

"Where are you going?" he says. "Wait, I have, like, a million questions!"

While still backing away, I hold up my finger warningly. Then I turn around, rush to the door, and grab my coat. Right before I leave, I hazard a glance back at Larson. He mouths the words "I'm sorry."

I fling the door open and get the hell out of there.

What is going on in the world anymore?

Ian Larson is a dickhead ass-face skeleton with dust bunnies the size of cats. He's not supposed to come through in the end and apologize for being a dickhead ass-face skeleton.

God, that makes me mad!

I'm able to sustain this anger most of the way home. But I take a small break from it to buy a large pizza from the good place with the mean lady to take home with me.

When I get to the park, those same drunks are smoking cigarettes on a bench while having a spirited argument. I'm tempted to jump in and take sides just to do something with this anger, but I don't speak Polish.

It's a cold, cold night and the streets are mostly empty. Eventually the anger dissipates, and I realize it was a convenient distraction from the agony of Ramie's absence, but it's not sustainable. In the end, I might have to accept that Larson *is* a decent guy after all. Shouldn't there be a silver lining involved in that revelation? Something about the world being a kinder place than Jill and I previously suspected? Why does it merely annoy me?

As I turn the corner onto Edgar Avenue, I begin to dread the approach of my empty apartment. Then I notice someone sitting on the front steps. His shoulders hunch forward against the cold, and he has a big blue duffel bag next to him.

My pace quickens.

Seeing me, he stands up.

I break into a sprint, then stop at the foot of the stairs. Guess who's sitting at the top, looking down at me.

Go ahead, guess. Come on, take a guess. Oh, forget it.

It's Tommy Knutson!

"Jack!" he says, like he's surprised to see me showing up at my own apartment. Then he walks down the steps toward me. "I've been calling for an hour. Don't you guys still have the same cell phone?"

I have to pause here to admit something sort of embarrassing. I'm so happy to see Tommy Knutson it's taking all of my willpower (and testosterone) to resist jumping up and down and squealing like a little girl.

"Is it okay if I crash here?" he asks. "I spent my last dime on that plane ticket."

"Defo," I say. I hand him the pizza box, then march right past him and pick up his duffel bag. "Come on."

He follows me up the stairs. "I had to get the subway from JFK," he says. "Do you have any idea how complicated that is?"

"Actually, I do."

When we get inside, I bring his bag to Ramie's room. "You can sleep in here," I tell him. "Don't mind Mannequin. She's cool. If you want, I can move her to my room."

Tommy looks around the mostly empty room. "Where's Ramie?"

"London," I say.

"Oh." He looks at me, expecting more.

But I don't feel like giving him any more right now. Not on that subject. "So, did you come because of that message from Jill?"

He nods. "I wanted to surprise her."

"Oh, she'll be surprised all right. Hey, do you need a shower or anything?"

"That would be awesome," he says.

I show Tommy how the shower works and get him some towels that are freshly folded if not exactly clean. Then I hit the kitchen and start doing some "maintenance."

When Tommy emerges from Ramie's room showered and dressed, he looks like a new man.

"That is a seriously good shower," he says. He cocks his head to the side. "Are you wearing a girl's scarf?"

"It's an ascot," I say.

He nods; then his eyes drift to the pizza box on the coffee table.

"Hungry?" I ask.

"Starved."

I bring some paper towels over to the coffee table, and we sit on the couch and silently scarf for a few minutes.

"So," I say. "Life on the road. Thumbs up or down?"

Tommy shrugs and wipes some sauce from his mouth. "Surprising," he says. "Enlightening. Productively lonely."

"Is that a poem?"

He laughs. "So you're all right, then? I got really worried when I got that text from you."

"I was just lonely," I tell him. "Plain lonely. Not productively lonely."

"I hear you," he says. He points to the window. "Hey, I think it's snowing. Want to go up to the roof?"

"It's kind of cold," I say.

He laughs. "You and Jill," he says. "Cold is a fact of life. You're from Massachusetts. When are you going to accept that?" He grabs his winter coat from the arm of the couch. "Come on. The view's amazing."

"I know." I get my coat and follow him out. "I live here, remember?"

When we get to the roof, I realize I haven't been up there since that time Ramie and I put on a sex show for the neighbors. The chair remains where we left it, broken and windblown into a corner.

Tommy heads straight around the water tower to look at the view of Manhattan. I follow him.

"Man," he says. "I don't care how long you live here, you could never get blasé about that view."

"Eh," I say. "Bunch of tall buildings, bunch of noisy people." I admit it feels pretty cool to act blasé about it. I stick my hands in my pockets and bounce on the balls of my feet to stay warm. The Manhattan skyline is pretty enough I guess, but I prefer the look of the snow. The streetlights make it sparkle, and the whole city seems to have hushed just to watch it.

"What are you guys doing for Christmas?" he asks. "Are you going home?"

"Probably," I say. "I guess it's up to Jill. What about you?"

"I have to convince my mom to buy me a plane ticket back to San Francisco so I can pick up my car. I left it at my cousin's."

"Or," I say, "you could just sell the car and stay here."

He looks at me.

"You know," I say. "Or whatever."

He nods mysteriously, then looks at the skyline again. "I like that idea," he says. "Hey, thanks for the pizza. Sorry I'm so short on cash."

"No worries," I say. "It's on Jill. She's rolling in it these days."

"Yeah?"

I nod.

Tommy rests his elbows on the roof ledge. "I really missed you guys."

I rest my elbows on the ledge next to him. "Yeah, we missed you too."

Tommy's eyes wander over the expanse of the Manhattan skyline, which still sparkles like a strand of jewels. I hope he does stay in Brooklyn. It'll be fun showing him around.

"Hey, Tommy?" I say.

"Yeah?"

I watch the glistening snowflakes falling downward to disappear. "Sorry I was such a jerk," I say.

"You weren't a jerk."

"Yes I was."

He shakes his head. "You were . . ." He narrows his eyes as he thinks about it. "A work in progress."

"Oh yeah?" I say. "You mean, like a half-sculpted statue of David?"

"Yes," he says. "That's exactly what I meant."

He's being sarcastic, but I like the idea. A colossus of manhood, that's me. "Hey, do you think I'm average-looking?"

He looks at me and laughs. "Jack, trust me. There's nothing average about you."

"But you mean that in a good way, right?"

He nods, then we both return to looking at the glistening things before us.

It seems impossible that I ever disliked Tommy Knutson. What's to dislike? He's a prince. For my money, he's the only guy in the world who's worthy of Jill's heart. I wonder if he knows that, or if I should tell him.

If this were Jill and Ramie, they'd have a long, teary confession about how wrong they were to be mean to each other and how friends have to always *always* forgive each other when they've acted like jerks. Then they'd hug and wipe their eyes and laugh and stuff.

Not Tommy and me. We just stare at the sparkling things

before us. I'm grateful he's my friend, and I feel foolish for not knowing he was all along. But I'll never say these things to him. I don't think I have to. I'm pretty sure he knows.

After a while we head downstairs, eat some more pizza, then hit the sack.

Before I kill the light, I think about how excited Jill's going to be when she wakes up to find him there. It'll be like Christmas coming early.

Hey, by the way, Jill, you've done a lot of cool things since we moved to New York but there's one thing you got wrong. There's no point in trying to separate love from sex. Maybe some people can pull it off, but you and I can't. For us, they belong together. There's nothing wrong with that. I'm saying this as your brother. I'm looking out for you, kid. You're not a sex machine. You're a love machine. When you give your body to Tommy Knutson, your heart's going to be there too. It's okay. He's worthy of it. So go for it, coyote or no coyote. And don't worry about me. I can handle it. I can handle a lot of things.

I pull the cord on the poodle lamp and slide down between the covers. As I watch the snow pile up on the windowsill, I realize I don't have to work so hard to become something more than Ramie's boyfriend. I already *am* more than that. I'm a brother. I'm a friend. I'm even a son.

I'm pretty good at it too. In fact, I'm the best brother, son, or friend you could ask for.

I'm Jack McTeague, for crud's sake.

(re)cycler

When I die, people will know my name. They'll say, that was Jack McTeague. He was Amazing and Wonderful. He was a Colossus of Manhood. Oddly, he had no birth certificate. Nevertheless, he was here.

Man, was he ever here.

Find out more about

Jack
&
Jill

on
Facebook.com

ACKNOWLEDGMENTS

Thanks to Mallory Loehr for her sharp insights, Jill Grinberg for her wise guidance, Scott and Justine for advice and support, Altered Fluid Writers Group for their depth of commitment, and the 'craft crew for camaraderie and snacks.

LAUREN MCLAUGHLIN grew up in the small town of Wenham, Massachusetts, about twenty miles north of Boston. After college and a short stint in graduate school, she spent ten "unglamorous" years in the film industry, both writing and producing, before abandoning her screen ambitions to write fiction full-time. She lives in Brooklyn, New York, with her photographer husband and is currently working on her next novel.

You can find Lauren's Web site and blog at
www.laurenmclaughlin.net.